THE SANIBEL SUNSET DETECTIVE'S LAST CASE

Also by Ron Base

THE
SANIBEL SUNSET
DETECTIVE'S
LAST CASE

RON BASE

West-End
Books

Library and Archives Canada Cataloguing in Publication

Title: The Sanibel sunset detective's last case / Ron Base.
Names: Base, Ron, author.
Identifiers: Canadiana 20210273933 | ISBN 9781990058035 (softcover)
Classification: LCC PS8553.A784 S28 2021 | DDC C813/.54—dc23

Publisher's Note: This is a work of fiction. Names, characters,
places, and incidents either are products of the author's imagination
or are used fictitiously. Any resemblance to actual persons,
events, or locales is entirely coincidental.

West-End Books
133 Mill St.
Milton, Ontario
L9T 1S1

Text design and electronic formatting: Ric Base
Cover design and coordination: Jennifer Smith
Sanibel map: Ann Kornuta

"I would come to her even if I had to wade through blood."
Iris Murdoch, *A Severed Head*

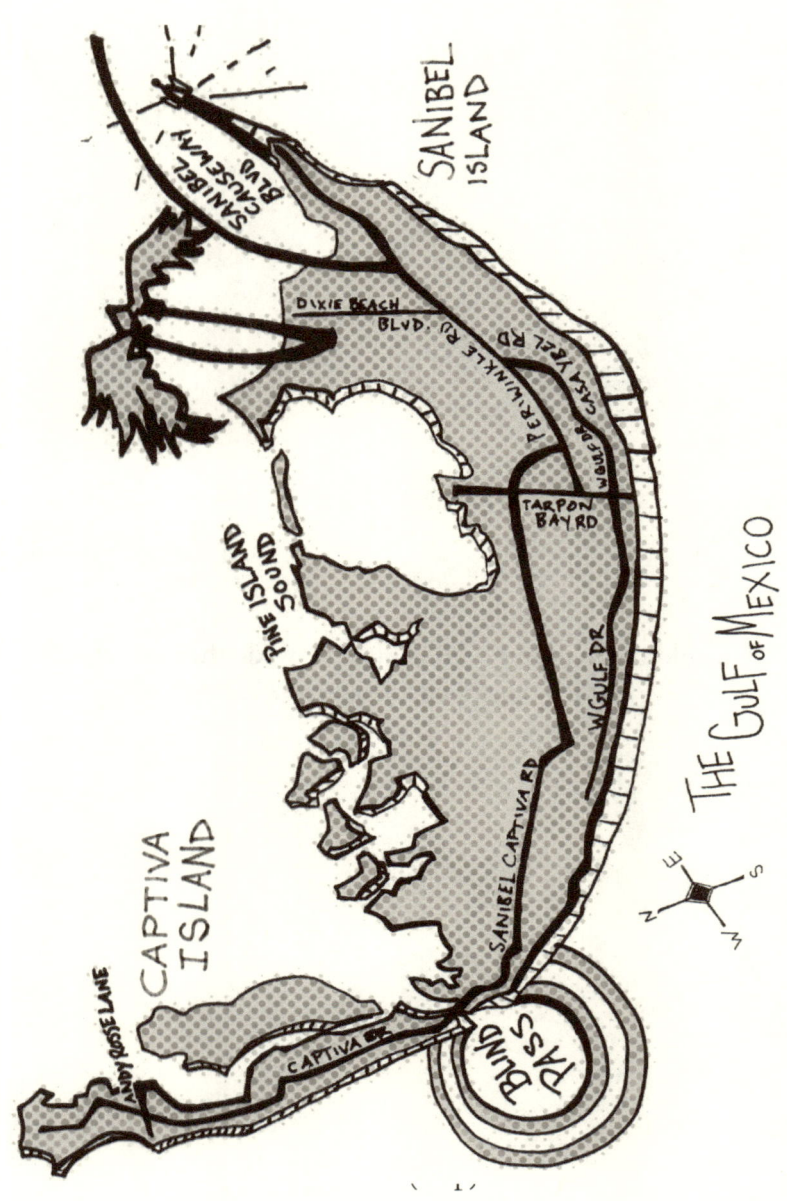

1

After the storm, before the chaos and uncertainty that was soon to follow, she called Tree Callister.

"Judy?" Tree said in disbelief when he answered the phone.

"Your first wife, in case you've forgotten," Judy said.

"How could I forget?" Tree said. He glanced at the woman who was now his wife, Freddie Stayner. She sat not far away in the lanai of the condo that they rented after the hurricane had rendered uninhabitable their house on Captiva Island. Originally, they talked about rebuilding, starting over again. That talk had soon drained away. The repairs were not possible. There was no energy for starting over, not on Captiva, anyway. Not on Sanibel where the Sanibel Sunset Detective Agency had been lodged in the back of Cattle Dock Bait Company. There was no bait company. There was no detective agency. There was only one tired and aging detective, a former Chicago newspaper reporter who probably should never have become a detective in the first place. After twenty years, Tree and Freddie had decided to leave Florida. Hail and farewell—but definitely farewell.

"I need to see you," Judy said. There was an edge of desperation in her voice.

"Is everything okay?"

"No, it is not. Otherwise, I would never call you."

That was true, Tree mused. Judy had never forgiven him for what she claimed he had done to her. A young Chicago woman who only wanted to be a suburban housewife with kids and a husband coming home every day at five o'clock, instead had ended up with a hard-drinking, unreliable reporter, who hardly ever came home, let alone at five o'clock.

So many years later, hearing her voice still sharply reminded him of his failed domestic past, and made him feel guilty about it all over again. Her voice also reminded him that getting involved with the dangerous woman who had become Judy Markov could lead to a whole lot of trouble. And more trouble, in the wake of arguably the worst hurricane in Florida history, was not something Tree needed right now.

"Tree?" Judy's tense voice interrupted his reverie. "Are you listening to me?"

"I'm not so sure that the two of us together is such a good idea."

"I don't care what you're not sure of, I need you—now." Judy sounded tenser than ever.

"Tell me," he said.

"Let's not talk on the phone."

"This doesn't sound good, Judy," Tree said in a warning voice.

"It isn't," Judy said.

Blunt and raw, Tree thought. Not at all like Judy—the duplicitous Judy, saying one thing in order to get to the other thing that she really wanted.

He stole another glance at Freddie. Her expression was steadfastly parked in neutral—as if waiting for Tree to once again fall down the rabbit hole.

Tree swallowed hard. "Where do you want to meet?"

Freddie did not look pleased.

They had moved to Sanibel because Freddie, the extraordinary woman who for some unfathomable reason had fallen in love with an unemployed former *Chicago Tribune* reporter not exactly thought of as dependable marriage material—just the opposite in fact.

Freddie had grown tired of the executive life at a big midwestern supermarket chain and to everyone's surprise, even her own, had decided to take a job running a small chain of Florida grocery stores headquartered on Sanibel Island.

As a child, Tree had vacationed on Sanibel with his parents. But he hadn't been to the island in years. It was the last place he imagined ending up. Tree was not quite certain what made him become a private detective, possibly reading too much Raymond Chandler and Dashiell Hammett, and, under bedcovers late at night with a flashlight, forbidden Mickey Spillane. He had devoured Bogart, the ultimate cool tough guy without a gun, in those velvety black-and-white movies he made in the 1940s. The difference was those detectives plied their trade on dark urban streets. They wore fedoras and looked great in trench coats. This was sunny Sanibel, a tourist paradise where nothing ever happened and where no one would look good in a trench coat. Everyone thought Tree was crazy, even Freddie. Well, everyone was wrong about one thing. Over the past twenty years plenty had happened to Tree. They were right about him being crazy—out of his mind, particularly at an age when most men were content to retire to a golf course or discover pickleball or go deep-sea fishing. Tree wasn't interested in any of those things. He preferred to almost get himself killed instead.

He had set up an office at the Sanibel Chamber of Commerce, his pal Rex Baxter being the organization's president. Tree and Rex had become friends in Chicago where Rex was the beloved weatherman on a local television station. Rex previously had been an actor in Hollywood, doing mostly bit parts in B-pictures. He had returned to Chicago to do an afternoon movie show before taking on the job of telling viewers when it would rain. What made Rex so popular was the fact he didn't know much more about when it would rain than his audience. How Rex had ended up on Sanibel and Captiva Islands as president of the Chamber of Commerce was a tribute to his ability to land anywhere and quickly befriend the natives, and soon cause them to love him unconditionally. Rex had left the area already, lured back to Hollywood, the town that had once so thoroughly rejected him. He had been reborn as a result of the Netflix series based on his memoir of his years in Hollywood. Harrison Ford had played the older Rex looking back on his life. A hot young actor named Jacob Elordi portrayed the youthful Rex.

Tree was missing his old, dear supportive friend. Gladys Demchuk, the former adult star known as Blue Streak who was supposed to help Rex with his memoirs and answer the office phone, had spent most of her time saving Tree's sorry derriere. Now she too was gone. She was on the run from the law, accused of murder—but that was another story, wasn't it, Tree thought sadly to himself. One of the many that hadn't worked out as he intended and had resulted in too much sadness.

Everything was gone, Tree reflected for the umpteenth time—his friends, his home, his business, a way of life—everything gone with a terrible wind.

Everything except Freddie. Thank God for her, he thought constantly. With her, he could continue. Without her?

He didn't even want to think of that possibility.

2

Tree could never entirely get his head around what Judy had become in the years since they had divorced.

She had met and then married a notorious Russian oligarch, Alexei Markov. This was back in the days when the oligarchs had access to the world, including the U.S. It was an unlikely marriage, to say the least, but before much final judgment could be passed, Alexei had died suddenly of a heart attack. Judy had inherited the international business that had made him one of the world's richest men.

It was assumed that Judy would not involve herself with her late husband's business affairs. There were, after all, many ruthless rivals for Alexei's empire. Judy would never be able to stand against them. She fooled everyone, quickly dispatching her rivals. Not only did she take command of her husband's empire she actually expanded it, and in the process, became known as the Dragon Lady.

"You're out of your mind agreeing to meet her," stated Freddie as soon as Tree got off the phone. "Particularly right now considering everything we have to deal with."

"It's only a meeting," Tree argued. "I'll see what she wants. Nothing more than that."

"That woman is poison," Freddie asserted. "And the poison seeps into you every time you encounter her."

"That's a bit over the top," Tree argued, thinking that in fact it probably wasn't really over the top at all.

"She works on your guilt about the marriage when she was someone else entirely—*you* were someone else entirely."

"A shitty husband," Tree said.

"She manipulates you," Freddie said vehemently.

"No, she doesn't."

Freddie gave him a look. A disdainful look, if Tree was reading her properly—and when it came to Freddie's disdainful looks, they weren't hard to read. "I hate to mention this, but as we decide what to do with the rest of our lives, post hurricane, you have stated that since the business, such as it was, is gone, it is time to move on."

"You will notice I haven't used the word retired," Tree said.

"Even so," countered Freddie. "Moving on should not include meeting your ex-wife to get into what is almost certainly going to be trouble that you don't need right now."

"The word obligation comes to mind," Tree said.

"So does the word, guilt."

"Look, I will drive out to Coral Springs and see what she wants. If it's anything dangerous, I will say no."

Freddie did what she usually did in the face of such pronouncements: she rolled her eyes.

"I don't like it when you roll your eyes like that," Tree said.

"It's either that or I wring your neck," Freddie said.

"Then I prefer the eye rolls."

Freddie did not give him an eye roll this time. This time it was a resigned shake of her lovely head.

Tree's phone began ringing. "I'm still in Hollywood, calling to make you jealous," Rex Baxter said as soon as he came on the line.

"That won't be hard to do today," Tree said. "What have you got?"

"I'm currently at the Bel Air Hotel getting a massage from

a delightful young woman before my luncheon meeting with Jerry Bruckheimer."

"I'm certainly jealous about the massage, given my various aches and pains these days. I'm not so certain about lunch with Jerry Bruckheimer. I'll leave that to you."

"I've gone very Hollywood," Rex said. "What pisses me off is that this didn't happen when I was a young man. I would have enjoyed it immensely back then, a dream come true. Now, I'm taking it for granted, which I shouldn't. Still, you'll be glad to know it's all gone to my head and I've become impossible to live with."

"You've always been impossible to live with," Tree said. "Hollywood won't change you no matter how old you are."

"In addition to calling to gloat, I'm also interested to know how my best friend in the world is doing as his end on Sanibel approaches. Where are you now?"

"Not on the island," Tree said. "Coming into Coral Springs."

"What are you doing there?"

Tree hesitated before he said, "If I tell you, you're going to yell at me."

"Tell me," Rex said. "I won't yell."

"I'm on my way to meet Judy Markov."

"What? Good God, Tree." Rex was as close to yelling as possible, given that he was in the midst of a massage at a posh Hollywood hotel that undoubtedly frowned on yelling.

"You promised not to yell," Tree pointed out."

"I'm not yelling, as more or less promised but I am asking as quietly as possible, whether you have taken leave of your senses."

"If you talk to Freddie, she would say that happened about twenty years ago."

"That ex-wife of yours is toxic," Rex said. "Every time you go near her, there is trouble."

"Interesting," Tree said. "Freddie used almost the same word."

"She's right. I'm right. You should listen to us."

"This is a courtesy call, nothing more. I want to make sure she's okay. I'm hearing Hurricane Ian destroyed her house. She's living in Coral Springs."

"Courtesy call?" Rex said disdainfully. "There is no such thing as a courtesy call where Judy is concerned. She wants something from you and that's never good—for you. Which I'm sure Freddie also told you."

"There's not much Judy can do to me at this point, we're packing up to leave."

"Just be careful," admonished Rex. "I'm sorry I'm not there to keep you on the straight and narrow."

"It's been a challenge over the years, but you've managed to do a pretty good job."

"Hey, I hate to admit it, but I actually miss you."

"I wish you were here," Tree said. "It's a very strange time. Ian. Deciding to move. You gone. Gladys disappearing."

"Yeah, Gladys." There was a wistful tone in Rex's voice. "I think about her a lot. Have you heard anything?"

"I get a visit from the FBI every so often demanding to know if I know where she is. Other than that, nothing."

"Listen, I gotta go," Rex interrupted. "Harrison Ford is on the other line. Keep in touch—and stay away from Judy."

And Rex was gone, leaving Tree curiously depressed. Had he lost his friend to massages at the Be Air Hotel and calls from the likes of Harrison Ford? He tried not to think that was the case.

Preoccupied thinking about Rex, he nearly missed the

gravel strip that ran off the curve of the street into a cul-de-sac hidden by masses of foliage. He didn't spot the house until he passed through the entrance into a wide yard. It was a one-story affair that looked as though it had been pieced together by a succession of owners over the years. It was not a house Tree would have expected the American oligarch version of Judy to occupy. But then times were tough for everyone post Ian, even for Judy.

The guards in black T-shirts and jeans stationed at the entrance suggested that Judy had a lot more to worry about than a hurricane. Only in Florida could a half dozen tough-looking young men stand around armed with semiautomatic weapons, and no one in the neighborhood seemed to bat an eye.

Judy met him at the door under the wary, watchful eyes of her guards. "Did you have any trouble finding the place?" she asked by way of greeting.

"A bit, yeah," Tree said. She was paler than the last time he had seen her, and the designer outfits had been discarded in favor of shorts and a T-shirt. Without makeup there was a scrubbed innocence about her that immediately made him wary. There was no innocent Judy, Tree reminded himself. Not for a long time.

"Come inside," she commanded. The spider to the fly, thought Tree.

Judy stepped aside so that Tree could enter a sitting room full of old furniture outlined in what was left of the sunlight that seeped through closed blinds. A lamp burned at the far end of the room, illuminating a kitchen. Cardboard boxes were piled everywhere.

Possibly taking note of his apparent confusion as she closed the door so that they were alone, Judy said, "Well, what do you think?"

"I'm wondering what you're up to."

"Trying to survive, like everyone else," Judy said. "I hear your place is gone."

"Looks like it," Tree said. "We're having trouble with insurance but then just about everyone is. What about you?"

"The storm and then a fire. There's not much left I'm afraid."

"A fire?"

"Intentionally set," Judy said. "I wasn't there, thank goodness."

"Who would set your house on fire?"

"Since I decided to remain in the U.S. when the Ukraine war started, and did not support Mr. Putin in the manner he was demanding, it is not hard to imagine."

"The Russians still have agents operating here?"

That produced the first of what Tree imagined would be the numerous scowls he always inspired during his encounters with Judy. Much had changed over the years since they divorced, but Judy had managed to cling to her disdain for him—a disdain, he noted, that didn't stop her from calling as soon as she had devised a new way for getting him into trouble.

"Honestly, Tree you are so naïve. The Russians are very much with us. The fire was a warning. If I cooperate, then I get to stay alive. If I don't…well, burning what was left of my house to the ground was probably just the beginning."

Tree hesitated to ask the obvious question, fearing what it would lead to. Judy, perhaps sensing this, headed him off. "You must be wondering what I have to do to cooperate."

"I am trying not to," Tree said.

"There's a piece of jewelry they want."

"Jewelry? What kind of jewelry?"

"Jewelry with a story," she said.

"And I suppose I'm about to hear it," Tree said.

"I'll give you the Wikipedia version." Judy hardly paused before she went on. "In 1922, four years after the death of Nicholas II and Alexandra Feodorovna, his wife and consort, and their five children, the Soviet government put on display the jewels the tsarina had collected over the years. Absent in the photograph taken of the display was perhaps Alexandra's most valuable piece, the pearl and diamond tiara she had worn on her wedding day. The Alexandra Tiara as it has come to be known. It was thought to have been lost or broken down for its priceless stones."

"Why do I suspect I'm about to hear that it wasn't."

"That's right." Judy frowned, disliking her irritating former husband anticipating the climax of her story. "My late husband Alexei somehow acquired it years ago before he met me. I had no idea of its value until his good friend Vladimir Putin discovered it was in my husband's possession."

"And he wanted it?"

"Putin did but he grudgingly accepted the fact that it was in my husband's hands. There were many reasons for him to let it go—reasons that evaporated as soon as Alexei died. I thought he might come after it then, but for whatever reason, he didn't. I stayed mostly in his good books, I suppose."

"What happened?"

"What do you think? Ukraine. The U.S. sanctions. My failure to show him unquestioning loyalty."

"And now Putin wants the tiara back," put in Tree.

"It's an essential part of Russian history, I am told. It should be returned to its rightful place in the motherland."

"I assume you don't want to give it to him," Tree said.

"Let's say I want something in return for my generosity. I'm afraid Mr. Putin doesn't see it that way."

"Where is this tiara now?"

Judy hesitated just enough to make Tree even more apprehensive. "It's at the house."

"No," Tree said.

He was rewarded with one of her disdainful looks. "You don't even know what I want."

"Yes, I do," Tree stated.

"What?"

"I'm not going to get the tiara for you."

Judy went over to a nearby table and picked up a manila envelope that she brought back and handed to Tree. "Twenty-five thousand in cash. All you have to do is drive out to Sanibel, pick up the tiara and bring it back to me."

"If it was that easy you wouldn't be paying me twenty-five thousand dollars."

"Yes, I would."

"I can save you the money," Tree said. "All you have to do is get it yourself. Or send one of your well-armed goons."

"I can't go myself or else I would," Judy stated. "Right now, it's too dangerous. But no one will suspect you, Tree, someone driving by and stopping to look at the remains of what was once a Sanibel Island showplace."

"I'm not going to do it." Tree was sure he had struck the right assertive note. Judy apparently didn't think so.

"Yes, you are." She sounded even more assertive, to Tree's ears. Judy so sure of everything; Tree, not so much.

"What makes you so sure?"

"Because if you don't help me, if you don't help the woman whose life you nearly ruined in Chicago, the woman you caused endless amounts of pain and heartbreak, when that woman is murdered by a Russian assassin, you will never forgive yourself."

"Knowing that it could be me murdered by a Russian assassin will help bring about your forgiveness, I suppose," Tree said.

"No one's going to murder you, I promise."

"Where is the tiara?" Was that a deep, resigned sigh he heard coming from him? It must have been him. It certainly wasn't Judy, her eyes agleam with the sense of impending victory, the victory that always seemed to be hers as she somehow always managed to force her will on him. If the anger over a betraying husband was never quite extinguished, neither, he had discovered, was the betraying husband's guilt.

"It's in a wall safe. I'll give you the combination. Trust me, it won't be hard to find."

"That's the thing, Judy, I don't trust you—and I don't want your money." He threw the manila envelope down.

She handed him a slip of paper. "The combination," she said.

3

Tree drove back along Estero Boulevard through the devastation of Fort Myers Beach. Everyone went for the easy cliché and said the area resembled a war zone, and now driving along Estero, that was the cliché that automatically came to mind. The ruined skeletons, all that was left of houses on either side of the roadway; the deserted swaths of land that had once housed mobile home parks; the great piles of debris that had yet to be collected. Times Square, formerly a funky shamble of colorful bars, restaurants and souvenir shops, lining a thoroughfare that ran down to the pier jutting into the gulf was gone along with the pier. The area had literally been turned into a parking lot—six dollars to leave your vehicle.

On the bridge off Fort Myers Beach onto San Carlos Boulevard, piles of wrecked shrimp boats like big twisted toys were visible to his right, not far from the remains of yet another decimated mobile home park.

Fort Myers showed fewer scars from the hurricane, but as soon as Tree crossed the jerry-rigged causeway to Sanibel—a miracle of engineering erected in three weeks—the evidence of Ian's fury was on full display. Malls and shops stood forlorn and deserted as did condo buildings constructed on stilts against the possibility of flooding, betrayed by storm surge that destroyed ground floor electrical; the iconic Bailey's General Store which had withstood the ravages of Florida weather since the 1920s, was a fenced-off shell that would have to be torn down. The trees along Sanibel Captiva Drive were brown and dead.

Just before Blind Pass, Tree turned off Pine Avenue onto

Coconut Drive and drove to Judy Markov's walled and gated mansion. Before the hurricane, its splendor had been hidden behind a high wall and masses of foliage. The hurricane had stripped away the foliage and torn apart much of the wall leaving the remnants of the house visible to the world. Tree parked in front of the twisted entrance gate that now hung open. The storm had exposed the home, the fire had reduced it to a blackened ruin.

Tree got out of the car and went through the gate, along the drive to the boarded-up entrance, then through decimated hedges to the infinity pool at the rear of the house. A thirty-foot pleasure craft had been thrown bow up on the beach below the pool. The pool itself was a blackened mess of sand and tree branches and, peeping out through the muck, bits and pieces of deck furniture. The sliding doors leading into the house were either twisted out of shape or pulled off their aluminum frames. Tree stepped into a wide sitting room stinking of charred wood, full of water-soaked and stained white furniture. The roof was destroyed revealing the blue sky.

Judy said the safe was located in what she liked to call the library. Tree suspected her taste in literature hadn't progressed much past Nora Roberts. Whatever her references, the books that had filled the floor-to-ceiling shelves now lay in soggy piles on the floor.

The safe supposedly was hidden behind a wall panel. Except it wasn't hidden. The panel had been popped open to reveal a gray safe. Its door was ajar. Tree peered inside.

"It's not in there," announced a voice.

4

The girl standing behind Tree couldn't have been more than twelve years old, not quite five feet tall in a striped top and a pair of white shorts. Her feet were clad in pink flip-flops that matched the pink purse dangling from her arm. A mass of brown curls framed a solemnly expressive face.

"What isn't there?" asked Tree, slowly turning to the girl.

"Whatever it is you're looking for," the girl answered reasonably.

"What's your name?" Tree asked. His eyes darted around, expecting someone else to emerge, asking himself what in the world this kid would be doing in a burned-out shell of a mansion.

"Why would you want to know that?" The girl cocked her head, inquisitively.

"You probably shouldn't be here alone," Tree said.

"Why not?"

"Are you alone?"

"Maybe," she said coyly.

"I haven't told you my name," Tree said, by way of changing the subject. "It's Tree Callister."

"I'm Alice," she reported. "You know, like *Alice in Wonderland.*"

"Except I don't think you're in wonderland, Alice. You should tell me why you're here."

"There is someone outside who wants to talk to you," Alice said solemnly.

"Who wants to talk to me, Alice?"

"My mother," Alice said.

The woman leaning against the red convertible Corvette was smoking a long cigarette. Her blond hair brought to mind a 1950s movie star. Her big sunglasses prompted thoughts of Jackie Onassis. Her white shorts fit tightly to her hips. The white linen blouse matched her shorts. Shoes with kitten heels were a bit incongruous for a flip-flop state like Florida.

"Mother," Alice broadcast, as though she didn't want to leave any doubt as to the woman's identity.

Mother responded by dropping her cigarette to the ground and using the toe of her kitten-heeled shoe to grind it out.

"This is Mr. Tree," said Alice. "He is looking for something."

It was hard to tell since her eyes were hidden by the Jackie O glasses, but the way the woman cocked her head made Tree think she was inspecting him speculatively. "Mr. Tree, eh?"

"And who are you?" Tree asked.

"Someone wondering what you are doing here," the woman retorted in the gravelly voice of a dedicated smoker.

"I'm a private detective. My name's Tree Callister."

"*You're* a private detective?" Her tone was one of disbelief, a not untypical reaction whenever Tree revealed what he did for a living.

"That's right," Tree said.

"No disrespect, but aren't you a little old for that sort of thing?"

"I'm retiring soon. This is probably my last case."

"And what case is that?" The woman removed her sunglasses to reveal eyes that were large and deeply blue and full of skepticism.

"That's confidential," stated Tree.

"Confidential," Alice piped up brightly, "I like that word." She looked at the woman. "You're often *confidential*, Mother."

"That's enough, Alice," the woman said distractedly. She replaced her sunglasses as though she had grown tired of the unobstructed view of Tree.

"How about you?" Tree asked.

"How about me?"

"What's your name."

"Dahlia."

"And like I told you, Mr. Tree, I'm Alice."

"That's enough, Alice."

"And what brings Dahlia and Alice here today?"

"That's confidential," replied Dahlia.

"It looks like we're all at a bit of an impasse as to what we're doing here," Tree observed.

Dahlia turned to her daughter. "Alice, why don't you wait for me in the car?"

"I don't want to," Alice said with a frown.

"That's enough, Alice. Do as you're told."

"I hate you," Alice said petulantly.

"Alice, that's more than enough."

Alice delivered a scowl before stomping off to where the Corvette was parked, and then yanking open the passenger door.

"That child," said Dahlia. "She's becoming quite a handful." She glanced at Tree. "I don't suppose you have a cigarette."

"I don't smoke," Tree said.

"Neither do I."

"You just asked me for a cigarette. You were smoking as I came out with Alice."

"You must be mistaken," said Dahlia.

"Yes, I guess so," Tree said, thinking it wasn't worth arguing with this woman.

"Let's return to the subject we were discussing earlier," Dahlia suggested.

"Good," agreed Tree. "Tell me what you are doing here."

Dahlia again removed her sunglasses apparently needing further proof of Tree's existence.

"I work out of Miami," Dahlia explained, holding the sunglasses between elegant fingers. "In Miami I'm known as the Red Dahlia." She paused for effect, although exactly what effect this was supposed to have, Tree had no idea.

"In certain circles," Dahlia continued, "I have a reputation as someone who can fix things. A fixer, if you will."

"If you're here to fix this house, it's going to be quite a job," Tree observed.

Dahlia gave him a look that bordered on contemptuous. She called out, "Alice!"

Promptly the Corvette's door opened and Alice leaned out. "What is it, Mother?'

"Bring me your purse, dear."

"No, Mother." Alice's tone was high-pitched. "You promised!"

"Alice! Do as you're told," Dahlia ordered crossly.

Alice got out of the car and came back to Dahlia. She straight-armed the purse in her mother's direction. "You *promised*," Alice repeated.

Dahlia responded by yanking the purse from her daughter. She opened it up and extracted a package of Marlboro cigarettes and a Bic lighter. "Back to the car, Alice," ordered her mother.

"Mother!"

"Alice! Do as you are told."

Alice heaved a melodramatic sigh and stormed away. The car door slammed shut.

Dahlia busied herself lighting her cigarette, managing at the same time to hold onto the pink purse. Once she had done that, she inhaled deeply and blew a cloud of cigarette smoke into the air. "That's better," she said. "Honestly, that kid can be such a brat sometimes."

"You should listen to your daughter," Tree said. "Smoking's not good for you."

"I'm quitting." Dahlia took another drag on the cigarette and then added more smoke to the air. "Now where was I?"

"You were starting to tell me how you fix things," offered Tree.

"Which brings me to why we are both here today," Dahlia said.

"That's interesting," Tree said. "Why are we both here?"

"A tiara." Followed by another blast of cigarette smoke.

Tree arranged what he hoped would be read as a look of confusion. "A tiara? What's a tiara?"

"Come on," Dahlia said impatiently. "We both know what I'm talking about. It's a crown worn by Tsarina Alexandra of Russia. It's supposed to be here."

"Is it?" Tree asked in all innocence.

"But it isn't."

"I'm not sure what you are talking about," Tree said, adopting his best guileless expression.

"You've been inside. You've seen the safe. The tiara isn't there."

"Maybe you got here first and took it," Tree offered.

That earned Tree another contemptuous look. "You think I'd be wasting my time standing here talking to you if I had it?"

"You say you fix things," Tree said. "Who are you fixing things for?"

"Let's say there's an interested party who will not be happy to hear that an old guy named Tree is poking his nose where he shouldn't poke his nose."

"Would your interested party happen to be the Russian government?"

"There you go poking your nose." Dahlia paused to contemplate her cigarette before dropping it to the ground and again using her shoe to grind it out. "I really do intend to stop," she announced distractedly. She shook her head and looked at Tree with something like sympathy. "Boy, are you stumbling into a dark hole you don't want to fall into."

"Is that what I'm doing?"

"Yeah, you are," she said, opening the little pink purse. She withdrew a small pistol and pointed it in Tree's direction. "Here's the thing. You seem like an okay kind of guy, and if what I'm thinking is correct, you've somehow got yourself mixed up with someone who is going to bring you nothing but grief, and won't be around much longer."

"I'm not mixed up with anyone," Tree argued. He didn't sound very convincing, certainly not to Dahlia. She frowned impatiently and then became more conciliatory. "Tell you what? Let's call this an information meeting. We both walk away, friends, you go back to whatever senior living residence you came from and forget about continuing along the path that brought us together."

"And if I choose to proceed along this path you're talking about?"

"Well, that's why I brought this gun along with me," Dahlia said, raising the weapon for emphasis.

"You're going to shoot me?"

"That's what guns are for, aren't they?"

Tree heard the door of the Corvette open. Alice was back

with a scowl. "Mother! You promised you *would not* do this."

"I'm not doing anything." Dahlia's big blue eyes held fast to Tree.

"Yes, you *are*," insisted Alice. "Waving that gun around again. You promised you wouldn't."

"Mr. Tree and I are just finishing our conversation." Dahlia opened the purse and dropped the gun into it. She looked at Tree. "Aren't we?"

"Apparently."

"Come along, Alice." Dahlia was suddenly all motherly business. "We must be off."

"I don't like it when you're like this," Alice said morosely. "So mean to people. It's scary."

"Get in the car, dear, and don't argue." Dahlia was opening the driver's side door as she spoke.

Alice gave a helpless shrug then strode to the car saying, "Mother, give me back my purse. Mother?"

5

Despite his best efforts not to let it get to him, it riled Tree no end that Dahlia took one look at him and concluded he lived in an assisted living facility. An old guy who could be dismissed with a couple of threats. Okay, he allowed as he drove back across the causeway, one of those threats included the waving of a gun under his nose. Not the first time. Over the years, working in Southwest Florida, he had become used to people threatening him with guns. Not many mothers, but given where he lived, he supposed it was a matter of time before a mother with a gun showed up.

Dahlia didn't carry on like anyone's idea of a mother. Neither would you pick her out of a crowd as a Russian agent. Which was probably the idea of being a Russian agent. It was hard not to suspect she was working for Russians who also desired the Alexandra Tiara. Judy had failed to mention either that there might be competition or the possibility that the tiara wasn't in the house. He should have known better. Where Judy was concerned nothing was ever simple. Or if it did start out that way, it soon got complicated—and dangerous. This time it was a mother with a daughter who carried mother's cigarettes and handgun in her pink purse.

Judy had a lot to answer for.

It took him the better part of an hour to get back to Coral Springs. By the time he turned into Judy's compound, it was nearly dark. There was no sign of the guards who had manned the entrance. The drive was empty. The house was dark. He knocked on the front door but no one answered.

"They ain't there," said a voice coming from behind him.

A white-bearded old man—well, maybe not *that* old, Tree thought, given his own age— stood with a small white dog on the end of the leash. The dog cocked his head inquisitively at Tree.

"I was just here a few hours ago," Tree said. The bearded man wore cargo shorts and a red "Make America Great Again" baseball cap. His T-shirt displayed an American flag.

"You with them?" The bearded man was looking him up and down, his bleary eyes full of suspicion.

"You don't happen to know where they went?"

"No idea. Lot of mysterious comings and goings the last few days. Dangerous looking fellas wandering around with AK-47s." His eyes narrowed. "You're not packing, are you?"

"Packing?"

"You carrying a gun?"

"Not me," Tree said.

The bearded man looked relieved. "Can't be too careful"

"I understand," Tree said.

"A couple of hours ago, the whole bunch of them packed up and went roaring off. Not sorry to see them go, if you want to know the truth. They were disrupting the neighborhood. Fellas with guns. Not good."

"You're right about that," Tree agreed.

"You know these people, do you?" The suspicion was back.

"I know the woman," Tree said.

"Deep state shit," mumbled the bearded man. "You sure that woman's not FBI?"

"I can't imagine she is." And then immediately he thought, Maybe she is. It would certainly explain how she stayed out of the crosshairs of American authorities all these years.

"Deep state bastards of some sort, that's for sure," the bearded man muttered.

"News to me," Tree said. "I'd better be going."

The bearded man stepped closer, blocking Tree's way. His eyes were small and fierce. "Maybe you're FBI."

"I'm a little old for the FBI don't you think?" Tree said.

"Guess you are at that." The fierceness in his eyes subsided somewhat. He stepped back.

"You're a bit paranoid," Tree suggested.

"It's America, friend. Everyone's paranoid. The only way you survive."

As Tree walked back to his car, the little dog started snarling and barking, possibly unconvinced that Tree wasn't part of the deep state.

Since they had abandoned the house they loved on Andy Rosse Lane and could no longer sit in the fading sunshine of their terrace listening to the sounds of the crowd gathered to watch the sunset down the road at the Mucky Duck, Freddie and Tree now had to confine themselves to the sunlight-challenged living room of their rented condo. The fine view of the man-made lake and the herons that gathered at twilight was a degree of compensation.

"What you are saying then is that Judy has disappeared." Freddie cutting to the chase after Tree had related the details of his encounter with Judy Markov and how she had convinced him to recover a Russian tiara—the Alexandra Tiara. Not only was there no tiara, but there was no Judy, either.

"She wasn't at the Coral Springs house and she's not answering her phone."

"And this so-called Alexandra Tiara, it wasn't at what was left of her Sanibel house?"

"Correct."

"And you were accosted by a mother and daughter who you believe are working for the Russians." Despite her best efforts, Freddie was having trouble hiding her skepticism.

"Well, the mother," Tree corrected. He had left out the part where Dahlia produced the gun from her daughter's purse. No need to upset Freddie any more than she already was.

"I was going to say something like I can't believe you once again got dragged into Judy's mess, but that would be a lie," commented Freddie. "I can believe it only too well because it's your ex-wife and she has dragged you into so much shit so many times before."

"It appears that Judy is not the only one who wants that tiara." Tree strained to make that argument.

"Yeah, right." Freddie wasn't buying. She shook her head in exasperation. "You get sucked in every time."

"I don't," he responded lamely, knowing full well that wasn't true.

"Now what?"

Always the question Tree could never answer satisfactorily, mostly because he didn't know himself. The mystery of the trouble he tended to get himself into.

"Tree, we're leaving Sanibel," Freddie said, leaning forward to emphasize her point. "We are leaving all of this behind us, Judy Markov in particular. It's over. Finished. Hurricane Ian blew everything away, including our lives here. Please, please don't do anything to jeopardize what we have both planned."

"I won't do that," Tree said, "but I am concerned about Judy."

"God, Tree, that's exactly what I'm talking about." Exasperation was replaced with anger. Not a good sign, Tree thought.

He was saved from having to make more unconvincing excuses by the sound of his cell phone.

"Did you get it?" demanded Judy Markov.

"Where are you?"

"Never mind that. Did you get the tiara?"

"It wasn't there. However, a woman who called herself Red Dahlia was."

"What do you mean it wasn't there?" Judy's voice was strained.

"The safe was open and empty."

"Dahlia," Judy breathed, "It must have been her. She must have taken it."

"I don't think so," Tree said. "She thought I had it."

"Do you?"

"What do you mean?" Tree could hardly believe what she seemed to be intimating.

"Maybe you have the tiara and you're just not telling me."

"Yeah," Tree said dryly. "Freddie's sitting here wearing it on her head."

"Fine," Judy said with a sigh. "Point taken."

"Somebody knew that the tiara was at your house. They had to know about the combination to the safe. The question is, who would have that information?"

Silence on the other end of the phone. "Judy?" Tree said finally. "Who else?"

"I don't know," Judy said in the uncertain tone that made Tree think she wasn't telling him the truth. Insofar as Judy was ever likely to tell the truth.

"What about Dahlia—or Red Dahlia as she calls herself. She says she fixes things. How does she know about the tiara?"

"Fixes things," Judy snorted contemptuously. "Dahlia is a bitch. She doesn't fix things, she destroys them."

"Then you know her?"

"What did she say to you?"

"She told me to stay away—probably good advice."

"That's all?"

"She said you weren't going to be around much longer."

"Ha!" chortled Judy. "That's what she thinks."

"How do you know her?"

"Dahlia Rostova. Russian-American. Her father was a Soviet thug. The family came here when Dahlia was three or four. She runs her father's business now that he's dead. A gang of cutthroats. She's a bitch. But a dangerous bitch. She has dreams of empire, taking over from me in this country. It's not going to happen but she does her best to undermine me."

"Is that why you're in hiding?"

"I'm *not* in hiding," Judy claimed angrily.

"She said she's working for people who want the tiara. I suggested those people might be the Russian government."

"It's *not* the Russian government."

"Then who?"

"Right now, that is of no importance," Judy said dismissively. "What's important is that you find the Alexandra Tiara."

"*Me?*" sputtered Tree. "Are you joking? I'm not having anything more to do with this."

"It's too late," Judy said decisively. "They know about you, Tree. You're in it whether you like it or not. If I'm not going to be around much longer, neither are you. The only way out for both of us is to find that tiara."

"They? Who is 'they'?"

"The people who are going to try to kill you."

"Russian people."

"If you must label them with a nationality, I suppose so, yes."

"You said Putin wanted the tiara."

"Among others," Judy said enigmatically.

"If you're trying to scare me, it's not working." When he knew full well it was.

"It should, if you had any brains."

"I can't believe you are doing this," Tree said.

"If you care at all about me—if you care about yourself and Freddie, you'll find that tiara."

"I must have missed the part about how I'm supposed to do it."

"I'll be in touch," Judy snapped.

And hung up.

6

Tree found himself on the broad fairway of a golf course. He began walking, not sure where he was going. The sun was hot. He began to sweat. The fairway doglegged to the right past a grove of trees, around to a green. A large man in a white Banlon shirt that emphasized his girth, concentrated on making a putt. Orange hair exploded from beneath the sides of a red baseball cap with "Make America Great" printed on it.

The Orange Man positioned his putter over a little white ball. With a smooth movement, he gently tapped the ball. It rolled toward the hole a few yards away. Two inches or so before it reached its destination the ball came to an abrupt stop. The man's florid face turned the color of his baseball cap. He cried out, "Shit!" He noticed Tree and scowled. "You ruined my shot!" he shouted accusingly.

"No, I didn't," Tree protested.

"Who the hell are you? What are you doing here?"

"I'm not sure," Tree said. "I think I'm lost."

"I missed my shot because of you," the Orange Man repeated. "How did you get past my security detail?"

"I didn't see any security," Tree said.

The Orange Man moved across the green, positioned himself again to strike the ball. This time it did what it was supposed to do and dropped into the hole. The Orange Man issued a grunt of satisfaction before he turned to Tree. "You haven't told me why you're here. Have you come to help me make America great again?"

"I don't think you need my help," Tree answered.

"I thought so," said the Orange Man, shoving his putter into his golf bag.

"Thought what?"

"As soon as I saw you, I knew it. You're a loser."

Somewhat miffed, Tree asked, "What makes you think that?"

"The look of you, to be frank. The way you slumped along, like a beaten dog. I don't like losers. I'm a winner. Winners don't like to be around losers. Why don't you get lost?"

"I'm already lost," Tree said.

"Losers are always lost," the Orange Man said disdainfully. "Winners know where they are going."

"I'm leaving Florida," Tree explained. "We've bought a place in Chicago. I guess I'm having mixed emotions about it."

"No emotions," the Orange Man said. "Emotions get in the way. Losers have emotions. Winners can't afford them."

"The older I get, the more emotional I've become. Everything seems to set me on edge."

"That's because you're a snowflake," the Orange Man said disdainfully. "A snowflake moving north where all the other snowflakes are."

"Before I leave, I should find that tiara," Tree said.

"Tiara?" The Orange Man had small eyes like tadpoles. They had narrowed warily. "What are you talking about?"

"My ex-wife is after me to find a tiara once worn by the tsarina of Russia and now Putin wants it or he's going to kill my ex-wife and possibly me too."

"Vlad?" The Orange Man's face burst with delighted recognition. "Vlad's a friend. Now there's a tough guy. I love him. You do what you're told or you're dead. An iron fist. That's the way it's done."

"I don't want him to kill my ex-wife, though."

"Then you'd better do as you're told, and find this thing," the Orange Man said. He grabbed the handle of the cart on which his golf bag was mounted. "What's great about Vlad, he says he's going to do something, he does it."

"Yes, I guess you're right," Tree said.

The Orange Man started off. "Vlad's a winner, like me," he called. "You're a loser. You'll never find that tiara. Your ex-wife's as good as dead. And so are you."

"No, it's not true—she's not going to die! She's not—" Tree sat up. He wasn't on a golf course, he was in his own bedroom. Freddie was in the doorway looking concerned. "Are you all right?"

"Bad dream, that's all."

"You were shouting that you don't want Judy to die."

"Was I?"

"You've had too many of these crazy dreams over the years," Freddie said. "I can't wait to get you away from here so that you quit having them," Freddie said.

"Do you think that will do it?"

"I dearly hope so. They have haunted your life ever since you became a detective."

Tree eased himself out of bed. He felt stiff and old.

"There's someone on the phone."

"Who?"

"No idea. All very mysterious. You'd better take it."

Freddie disappeared from the doorway.

Tree pushed himself slowly to his feet, letting out an involuntary groan as he did, once again recalling Leonard Cohen's observation about aching in the places where he used to play. Truer words, Tree thought, shaking off the remnants of his dream—nightmare? In his shorts and a T-shirt, straightening out the morning kinks in his aching body, he made his way into the living room. Freddie handed him his cell phone.

"Mr. Tremain Callister?"

"Yes?"

"Mr. Tremain Callister my name is Sergei Markov. I am the young brother of the late Alexei Markov. It is imperative we talk as soon as possible. It is a matter of life and death!"

"I didn't know Alexei had a brother," Tree ventured.

"There was also a sister," said the voice on the phone. "Alas, Valentina is no longer with us. I am the only surviving member of the great Markov family. It is a position I take most seriously."

"What is this matter of life and death you talked about?"

"We should not talk of such things over the phone," Sergei said. "We must meet in person."

"I'm not sure that is a good idea," Tree said with a quick glance at Freddie. She was shaking her head vehemently.

"It is fine. I am sending a car for you." As though a free ride was the answer to any reservations Tree might have.

"Another not-so-good idea," Tree said.

"Listen, please, Mr. Callister, for your safety and that of your wife, you should do as I suggest. We meet, we talk, no problem."

"I don't know whether I mentioned it, but I don't like to be threatened."

"Of course, no threats." Sergei sounded hurt. "This is not a matter of threats but, as I said before, a matter of life and death."

"My death?"

"Not your death Mr. Callister—your *life*."

Tree paused to shoot Freddie another glance. She was frowning. "When would this car arrive?" Freddie's frown deepened.

"The car will arrive promptly at five o'clock. It will be driven by a man named Dimitri. Very efficient. A good driver. He will bring you to me. You may stay on your phone with your wife. If there is any problem, she will be able to call the authorities. All very simple and safe."

"You still haven't told me what this is about," Tree said.

"Dimitri will come for you at five. I look forward to our meeting."

Sergei rang off. Tree looked at Freddie. "You are not going to do this," she said in her most authoritative, no-nonsense voice.

"I don't think I have much choice."

Freddie regarded her husband with consternation. "Are you serious? The choice is *not* to go. Do *not* get yourself involved with this man—a man incidentally who may not even be who he says he is."

"On the other hand," reasoned Tree, "if I don't go, we could have this character harassing us. Let's see what Sergei wants. Like he said, I'll keep my phone open. You stay on the line with me. If anything happens, you'll know where I am and can call the police."

"I don't like this one bit," said Freddie sullenly. "We are supposed to be getting out of here, leaving all this behind. Now suddenly you are in deeper than ever."

"We *are* getting out of here, we *are* leaving all this behind us," Tree stressed. "But let's leave knowing Alexei Markov's brother isn't trailing after us."

"Do you really believe that?"

"Let's not take any chances," Tree said.

Freddie threw up her hands in despair. "I don't know what to say to you, Tree. I honestly don't. You seem determined to get yourself killed. Why is that? So you don't have to leave Sanibel?"

"Believe me, I want out of here—and don't worry, I'm not going to get killed."

"Every time you say don't worry," said Freddie with a grimace. "That's when I start to really worry."

7

The car did not arrive at five o'clock. It got there at five minutes to five, a black Mercedes. Dimitri turned out to be a squat little man, bald headed, with a growth of beard possibly to hide a weak chin. The camouflage didn't work.

"Enter please," Dimitri said in a deep, guttural voice as he held the rear passenger-side door open for Tree. "Nothing bad gonna happen."

If that was supposed to be reassuring, thought Tree, it wasn't. Dimitri looked like the guy you brought in when you wanted bad things to happen. The last thing he saw as the Mercedes pulled away was Freddie, any emotion she was feeling hidden behind dark glasses that made her look as though she couldn't care less. It crossed his mind that maybe at this point, she couldn't. Tree tried not to think of the nasty outcomes that had taken place over the years when he had failed to listen to her advice.

He thought for sure Dimitri would throw a hood over his head. But Dimitri kept his eyes on the road and said nothing about a hood or anything else. It became apparent as the Mercedes turned onto I-75 that they were headed in the direction of Naples. Along the highway there was no sign of the sort of devastation that decimated Sanibel and Fort Myers Beach. Florida continued to be the Florida of strip malls and car dealerships lined up on either side of the roadway.

"Can you tell me where we are going?" Tree called to Dimitri.

He didn't answer. Tree tried again. "Did you hear me?"

"I heard you," he answered gruffly.

"Can you say where we are going?"

"No."

The rest, for the next forty minutes or so, was silence until Dimitri approached the dune-colored plinth announcing Naples Municipal Airport in big black letters. "I am not getting on a plane if that's what you have in mind," Tree sounding a lot more concerned than he might have intended.

Dimitri said nothing. He kept the Mercedes pointed toward the two-story main terminal building.

"Dimitri? Did you hear me?" Tree called.

Dimitri stayed silent as he swung onto an asphalt road. Ahead, Tree could see dozens of private jets, their white fuselages glistening in the Florida sun, lined up in two rows adjacent to a runway.

He brought the car to a stop near one of the largest jets in the line. He turned off the engine and got out and came around the car to open the passenger door for Tree. "Out," he ordered brusquely.

Tree didn't move. The heat of the afternoon was like a blow delivered into the car's cool interior. "I want to know what's going on."

"You are such a baby," said Dimitri in a burst of exasperation. "No one is going to hurt you, big baby."

Tree preferred to be thought of as a tough guy who couldn't be pushed around. But that obviously wasn't Dimitri's impression. Tree got out of the car, bristling. "I'm not flying anywhere," he said lamely.

Dimitri indicated boarding stairs to the jet's open hatchway. "Go up there." Tree didn't move. He wasn't a big baby, but he told himself that he was careful and that had nothing to do with being a big baby.

"Come along," Dimitri said impatiently. "Mr. Markov, is a busy man. He does not have time to waste on babies." Tree pictured himself attacking Dimitri, delivering a series of mixed martial arts blows out of a John Wick movie that would convince his calcitrant chauffeur he was no one's baby. But then reality told him it would be a whole lot easier and safer to simply go up those stairs.

The woman who met him at the hatchway had waist-length honey-colored hair, and full pouty lips. She wore a short violet dress that stopped in time to show off knee-high black leather boots. It crossed Tree's intrigued mind that the boots were a little hot for the Florida weather, but maybe this woman never left the jet's cool interior. Given the luxury of the cabin, he could hardly blame her. He too would wear black boots and never leave the plane. Perhaps this woman might keep him company.

He shook off the thought. The big plush cabin was done in elegant grays. The tall, tanned muscular individual who greeted Tree seemed the perfect sort you would find with a long-haired woman in black boots on a hot day aboard a luxury jet.

"Look who's finally here," the muscular man said with a smile so white it was all Tree could do to stop himself from squinting. "You've met Stoya?"

"I haven't even met, you," Tree said. Stoya squeezed past and went to the muscular man and placed her hand on his arm, as though to claim him as her own. She wore green nail polish, he noticed.

"I am Sergei Markov, the man you suspect might kill you," he said with cheerful enthusiasm. "Tell him, Stoya. Reassure our friend that I do not kill people."

"Sergei is a lover, not a killer," Stoya confirmed. To emphasize the point, her long fingers with their green-painted nails, tightened on Sergei's arm.

"There, you see? The word from someone who knows. So now, won't you have a seat so that we can talk?" Sergei indicated one of the lounge chairs. As Tree settled in uneasily, Stoya plopped herself down in front of him. She crossed her boot-clad legs in a way that made him take notice. "What can I get you?" Sergei was saying. "Something to eat? Drink?"

"I'm fine, thanks," Tree said.

"Caviar, maybe. From Astrakhan in the Volga region, the best in Russia. The finest in the world."

"No thanks," Tree said.

"You know what they say in Russia, it isn't a party without caviar."

"Is this a party?"

"Leave Mr. Callister alone, darling," chimed in Stoya, leaning forward slightly and keeping blazing green eyes that matched her nails trained on Tree. She added, "Mr. Callister is a rather attractive older man." Tree couldn't help but be disappointed that Stoya had used the word "older."

Sergei dispensed a pleased laugh as he settled beside her. "Perhaps, darling," he said softly, "you might give Mr. Callister and me a few minutes."

"Of course, darling," Stoya purred. "Although you are a very mean person to push me away from such an attractive man."

"I am terrible, no question," admitted Sergei good-humoredly.

Stoya gave Tree a look that could easily be described as alluring before rising gracefully and swaying off. Sergei watched her progress, pleased. "She is something is she not, my Stoya? The love of my life, she is." He winked at Tree. "This month. So many beautiful women in the world, Tree, although I suppose in these conservative times, one must be a little more careful, discreet, one must say."

"What's this all about?" Tree demanded. "Why am I here?"

"What do you think of this plane, eh? Something else, eh?" Sergei was leaning forward, his eyes alight with excitement. "This is the Bombardier Global 5500, best in its class. First class. Very high end. It has Nuage seats. No one else has Nuage seats."

"I'm not flying anywhere with you, Sergei, if that's what you're getting at."

Sergei's eyes popped with delight. He chuckled. "My friend, what do you think? I am going to whisk you off to Russia? I make you disappear into the snowy depths of the Gulag?"

"The possibility crossed my mind," Tree allowed.

Sergei sat back chortling with laughter, as though that was the funniest thing he had ever heard. "Rest assured my friend, this plane will not leave the ground. Given the current situation in the East, the hatred of the Americans for my beloved country, better to leave it where it is." He waved his hand around. "For the time being this is my home."

Sergei leaned further forward so he could tap his forefinger against Tree's knee. "You must have a great deal of money for a plane like this—am I right?" When Tree didn't say anything, Sergei pressed, "Am I right or not?"

"I suppose so," Tree said reluctantly, not having any inclination to encourage him.

"Okay, I have the kind of money that gets you a plane like this. I could buy something bigger, no problem, but for me, this is fine. Women like Stoya, they love it. Okay?"

"What's the point, Sergei?"

"I must tell you this was actually my brother's plane. The bastard dies, he leaves me a plane. Well, that's okay because his pal Vlady, he's my pal too and I'm gonna get Alexei's business despite what his American widow thinks."

"You mean Judy Markov," Tree interjected.

Sergei's face darkened. "How could I know? Vlady wasn't such a pal after all. Who gets my brother's business? The widow, says Vlady. Why he decides this I'll never know. Big mistake. But there it is. It's Vlady. If I don't want to meet a bullet walking down a Knightsbridge Street, I'd better go along. And I do."

"I still don't know where any of this is going or what it has to do with me," Tree said.

"Patience, Mr. Callister. Patience. I am a patient man, and sure enough my patience has paid off. Vlady is now my friend. Judy, my dear sister-in-law, she is no longer Vlady's friend. A failure of loyalty I suspect."

"Because of Ukraine," Tree added.

"Not a word I like," Sergei said after a silence. He ceased his tapping on Tree's knee at the same time as he dropped his voice. "Here is the thing, Mr. Callister, given recent events on Sanibel, the terrible hurricane, a resulting fire that destroyed what was left of her house, Judy Markov has disappeared. It is most necessary that I find her."

"I'm afraid I can't help you with that," Tree said, beginning to understand what all this was about. "Judy and I haven't been together for a long time."

"Ah, but you see, I believe you can be a great help," responded Sergei. "You are, I am told, a detective in the area—a private investigator, if you will."

"I'm retired," Tree said. "In fact, I'm leaving Florida."

"What's more, even though it was, as you say, a long time ago, you are the first husband of my brother's wife. You have the inside track, so to speak, as to her thinking and where she might be."

"I have never been able to understand Judy's thinking,"

Tree pointed out. "And I have no idea where she might be." True on both counts, Tree thought to himself. "Besides, if Vlady, as you call him, is now your friend, why would you have to get in touch with her?"

"There are certain things that must be discussed."

"Well, like I say, there's nothing I can do to help you."

"You see, Mr. Callister, I am somewhat at a loss here in Southwest Florida. I am in need of assistance from someone familiar with the area. You are that person, Mr. Callister. I am afraid I must insist. It is most imperative I have communication with Judy Markov."

"I'm still not convinced you're giving me the full story," Tree said. "I can't believe the only reason you want to find Judy is to deliver warm greetings from your pal, Vlady."

"Yes, there is more to it." Sergei permitted himself a capitulatory smile. "As it happens, my sister-in-law has an item desired by my dear friend. An item that should not have been in her possession in the first place. Although I am now friends with my friend, I am told we will be even better friends if I can return this item to him. First of all, however, I must locate Judy. That is where you come in, Mr. Callister."

As Tree started to object again, he was cut off by Sergei's sharply raised hand. "Please, before we continue, I must beg your indulgence for a few minutes." He rose abruptly from his impressive Nuage chair. "Please remain where you are. I will return shortly."

No sooner had Sergei disappeared then Stoya reappeared, holding an envelope. The black boots shone in the overhead light.

"You must be warm in those," Tree observed.

"In what?" Stoya looked confused.

"Those boots."

"Silly man." She bent down to him. She smelled wonderful, Tree thought vaguely as she kissed him on the lips. Before he had a chance to object—he was certain he was about to object—she pulled away. "A most attractive silly man." The purr had returned to her voice. She dropped the envelope onto his lap. "This is for you." Tree stared down at the envelope. "My Sergei is a very generous man," Stoya went on in a tone that contained less of a purr and was more businesslike. "Very generous but also a man used to having his way. He can also be a dangerous man when he does not get his way."

"Are you dangerous too?"

"I am dangerous in other ways," she said. "Why I usually get *my* way. If I were you, silly attractive man, I would do as he asks."

"I should talk to Sergei," Tree said, still trying to process Stoya's kiss.

"Sergei is on a most important call to Moscow," Stoya said. "The same time each day. He is no longer available. He will be in touch to check on your progress. I will see you out."

"I'm not taking the money," Tree said.

"Please." She pushed the envelope into his hands. "I will be in trouble if you don't." Her face had become solemn.

Who could resist Stoya? Tree took the envelope.

Dimitri was waiting for him at the bottom of the flight stairs. "You see?" he said. "No one made you fly anywhere and you are still very much alive."

"For now," Tree said.

"For now?" Dimitri waved his hand in the air. "That is all any of us can say. We are all doomed."

8

"Stoya kissed me," Tree said.

Freddie, finished counting the hundred-dollar bills that were in the envelope Stoya had given him. "There's fourteen thousand dollars here," she said with something like astonishment. "This guy simply handed you fourteen thousand dollars."

"Actually, it was Stoya," Tree corrected. "She called me a very attractive man."

Freddie put aside the cash she had arranged in stacks long enough to give him a look. "Tree, she was trying to manipulate you. Do you really believe that a young woman, Russian eye candy if you will, wearing black leather boots in Florida, for heaven's sake, is doing anything else?"

"I wouldn't exactly call her eye candy."

"Stoya dazzled you, flattered you, manipulated you, and here you are home with fourteen thousand dollars you should not have taken from someone who is probably a Russian gangster."

"Sergei didn't say it in so many words, but it's hard to believe he isn't after the Alexandra Tiara."

"But you're not going to get dragged into this any more than you already have," Freddie said with certainty.

"What choice do I have?"

"Tree, for God's sake, do we have to go over this again? Your choice is to give back the money and not have anything more to do with this nonsense. Besides, do you have any idea where Judy is?"

"No," Tree admitted.

"Then what chance do you have of finding her before we leave?" Freddie didn't wait for his answer. "None, I would say. Therefore, you should give the money back." She didn't so much look as scowl at him, daring him to contradict her.

"You're right...I suppose," Tree said grudgingly.

"Take it back." A statement.

Tree stared at the money, mulling over what to do. His phone rang.

"Have you found the tiara?" Judy demanded as soon as she came on the line.

"Where are you?"

"Never mind where I am. Have you got the tiara or not?"

"We need to talk."

"No, we don't," Judy said. "Just answer my question."

"Not over the phone."

"Don't be an ass, Tree."

"Judy, I will be in the parking lot at the Edison Mall in Fort Myers tomorrow afternoon at two o'clock. Meet me there. Otherwise, I'm not having anything more to do with you."

Tree hung up, immediately feeling better. There, he thought, no more putting up with Judy's nonsense. Taking initiative. Being assertive.

"I'm not sure what any of that accomplished," Freddie said, immediately taking the air out of his balloon.

"I'll show up, she won't, and that will be the end of it," Tree said, fighting to retake the high ground that he could never reach in debates over his relationship with Judy.

"Unless she shows up."

"Then I'll deal with it," Tree said halfheartedly.

Freddie pointed to the money on the table. "What about Sergei Markov?"

"I'll deal with him, too."

Freddie did not look convinced.

The parking lot at the Edison Mall, baking under the intense heat of the afternoon sun, was full of shimmering white vehicles. Freddie's black Mercedes was an anomaly amid all the white.

Even with the air-conditioning cranked full blast, the interior was beginning to overheat. Tree started to do what he usually did when he was on a stakeout, he began to feel drowsy. He put his head back against the seat. He would rest his eyes. For a moment...

The next thing he knew, a car door slammed and that jerked him awake. Judy sat in the passenger seat, smirking. "Some detective you turn out to be," she sneered. "Sleeping on the job."

"I'm not on the job and I didn't think you would come," Tree answered, straightening, shaking himself awake.

"I'm here," she pronounced. "What have you got for me?"

"You never told me that your late husband has a brother."

Judy was, Tree noticed with some satisfaction, taken aback. "What's he got to do with anything?"

"Are you aware that he's in Florida?"

"He's not in Florida."

"I visited with him yesterday on his jet at the Naples airport.

"You can't be serious," was Judy's response.

"I am."

"What could he possibly want with you?"

"He's anxious to hire me."

"To do what?"

"Find you."

She studied him as if searching for signs that this might be some sort of elaborate joke.

Tree broke the silence: "Sergei tells me you have fallen out of favor with Vlady. He is now Vlady's friend. He plans to take over your business but first of all, he must cement his relationship and to do that…"

"What? Find me? Is that it?"

"It's the Alexandra Tiara that he's after, unless I miss my guess."

"What have you done, you bastard?" Judy said angrily. "You lured me here. How long before Sergei shows up?"

"Come on Judy, give me a break. Do you really think I want to get you killed?"

"I don't know. Do you? And what makes you think Sergei wants me dead?"

"Does he?"

She shrugged. "Sergei is a mean bastard," Judy said. "He's been jealous of me ever since Alexei died. He thinks I've got the empire he should have."

"What are you going to do?"

Tree was certain he could hear the wheels turning in her head as she wrestled with the question. The air conditioning wasn't helping the atmosphere inside the car. It was hotter than ever.

"There's only one thing to do—we've got to find that tiara," she declared finally.

"I don't like you using the word 'we,'" Tree said.

"I'm paying you a lot of money to help me," Judy said.

"I told you, I'm not taking your money," Tree shot back."

"What about Sergei? I'll bet he's also given you a pile of cash."

"I'm giving it back."

Judy gave him a skeptical look. "Why would you do that?"

"He wants me to find you. I don't want him to find you."

"Oh, dear, if I didn't know better, I could start to believe you actually care."

"I do care, for God's sake, Judy."

"Then help me."

Tree exhaled loudly. "What do you want me to do?"

"Go back to Sergei." Judy was speaking fast. "Tell him that thanks to brilliant detective work, you have tracked me down. But I don't have the tiara."

"How is that going to help?"

"Hopefully, it will take some of the heat off me, at least for the time being."

"I'm not sure he will believe me," Tree said.

"Do you have a better idea? Besides, you say you want to return the money he gave you. This gives you the chance to do it. I hate to say this, but right now you're about the only friend I've got." Judy added grimly, "I think that tells you all you need to know about the state of things."

"Okay," Tree nodded. "I'll go back to Sergei."

"God, it's hot in here." She opened the door to admit a blast of heat.

"Hold on," Tree said as she started out. "How do I get in touch with you?"

Judy was out of the car before she said, "I'll be in touch with you." She shut the door, cutting off the incoming hot air.

9

"I didn't know they let losers in the steam room."

In the rising heat, the sweat poured down the Orange Man's puffy red face. His orange hair was plastered against his head. He was naked, slumped against the white tiles, steam swirling around him.

Tree, sitting across from him, was also naked. Did they not supply towels in steam rooms? he wondered.

"I hear you got paid off by a Russian," the Orange Man sneered. His eyes were closed. He couldn't be bothered to even look at Tree as he spoke. "How much did it take to pay you off?"

"Fourteen thousand dollars," Tree said. "But I'm giving it back."

"Chump change." The Orange Man pried his eyes open long enough to squint at Tree as though he might not otherwise believe what he was hearing. "God, you really are a loser, aren't you? Losers sell out cheap. Winners take it all."

"I wouldn't say that makes you a winner," Tree ventured.

"That's why you're a loser. Why you can be bought for a lousy fourteen grand. I wouldn't walk across the room for fourteen grand, let alone give it back."

A woman emerged through the clouds of steam. Stoya, too, was naked. She paused when she saw Tree. Her lips curled into a smile before she turned to the Orange Man. She sat and embraced him. "It was me," Stoya announced in that familiar purr of a voice. "As soon as Tree saw me, he couldn't resist. He took the fourteen thousand dollars."

"You couldn't buy me for fourteen thousand dollars," the Orange Man said with a mocking laugh. "You couldn't even get me on the phone."

"With you, my darling, I would know better than to even try." She snuggled against the Orange Man at the same time as she delivered a sly look in Tree's direction. "But him, well, I was wearing those black leather boots…"

"I love those boots," said the Orange Man.

"He was a pushover," Stoya purred.

"I'm not a pushover," Tree cried.

"A pushover and a loser," chimed in the Orange Man.

Stoya looked at Tree and began to laugh. The Orange Man joined her. The two of them laughing together at Tree.

Laughing and laughing. Uncontrolled laughter…

Tree jerked awake. Freddie entered the bedroom. "You were yelling that you're not a pushover," she said calmly.

"Crazy dream," he said, taking deep breaths.

"Too many crazy dreams," Freddie said. "It's time you changed a few things—like what you're doing with your life."

"I agree," said Tree, easing himself off the bed. "I'm taking that money back to Sergei."

"When do you plan to do that?"

"Today."

"Good," Freddie said with satisfaction. "Maybe you're finally coming to your senses."

Tree wondered about that. He had been coming to his senses for a such a long time without ever getting there.

By the time he pulled himself together and started back for Naples, it was close to noon. Freddie had shoved his ill-gotten gain into a Publix shopping bag. He glanced at it on the passenger seat as he approached the airport, beating himself up all over again for getting into these messes. The Orange Man who came to him in the dead of night accused him of being what he feared most, a loser. The naked Stoya said he was a pushover, just about as bad as being a loser. She could be right. One kiss and that was enough. He walked away with the fourteen thousand she had slipped into his waiting hands. Well, he was about to make at least partial amends for his multitude of weaknesses.

Or he liked to think he was.

Blocks from the airport, preoccupied, Tree at first missed the plume of black smoke rising into the brilliant blue afternoon sky. There were masses of fire and police emergency vehicles at the gate, police officers directing traffic. Tree swung down a side street, parked, and then headed back to where a crowd had gathered at the chain-link fence. Peering through the fence at the billowing black smoke, Tree could make out the private jets lining the tarmac. The arcs of water from firehoses were trained at the far end of the line.

"Any idea what happened?" Tree asked a bearded man wearing a red MAGA baseball cap.

"An explosion is what I'm hearing."

A timid voice behind him said, "Please, let's get out of here." He turned to find Stoya standing behind him. She wore white shorts and a blue off-the-shoulder blouse.

"Stoya?" was all he could think to say.

"Don't just stand there with your mouth hanging open," she ordered in a low voice. "We must move quickly."

Before he could say anything, she started away, the crowd automatically parting for her. The bearded man in the MAGA hat gave him an envious glance. "Looks like you've got your work cut out for you, pardner."

Tree followed her in a daze of confusion, taking her arm as he caught up to her. "Where's Sergei?"

She looked at him with blank green eyes. "He's dead," she said in a monotone. "And you will be too if you do not get me out of here."

10

Stoya moved the Publix bag she found on the passenger seat as she slid into the car. "Grocery shopping?" she inquired as Tree started the engine.

"How do you know Sergei is dead?" Tree asked as the car moved forward.

"Because he was on his beloved plane when it blew up."

"That's where all the smoke is coming from?"

Stoya nodded.

"What happened to you? Why weren't you with him?"

"I became angry with Sergei, he was acting like a nasty beast. I decided to leave and look for the new Miu Miu shoes I've had my eye on. Sadly, they were sold out of my size. I returned as the plane exploded. It really was terrible. Poor Sergei." She didn't sound all that broken up by her boyfriend's death.

"Who would have done this?"

"Who else?" Stoya said with a shrug. "That wicked witch of the south—Judy Markov. Now I believe she will be coming after me. That is why you must save me."

Tree had his doubts about Judy's involvement in the explosion. What's more he had no idea how he could save Stoya. "Where would you like to go?"

"What are you talking about?" Stoya said in alarm. "You will take me where you can protect me. You have been paid a great deal of money to do this."

"And here I thought I was paid to find Judy."

"Now you do not find her," Stoya ordered. "Now you save me."

"Any ideas how I'm supposed to do that?"

"I have nothing, do you understand?" Stoya was abruptly the fragile damsel in distress. "Everything was on that plane with Sergei. My clothes. My money. Everything." Stoya had turned to him, imploringly. "You must help me. There is no one else!"

"Okay, okay," Tree said reluctantly. "I'll take you to my place in Gulf Harbour. We'll figure out something from there."

The distressed damsel disappeared. "Your place? Gulf Harbour?" Stoya's expression had become speculative. "Yes, they will not suspect I would be with you. I will be safe there."

"But safe from whom?" Tree asked.

"Like I told you. That terrible Markov woman."

"And suppose it isn't her?"

"Then I am in more trouble than I could have ever imagined," Stoya said forlornly.

To Freddie's credit—maybe it was her long experience with the unexpected where Tree was concerned—she didn't overreact when he walked through the door, Stoya trailing behind. There was instead a show of concern as Tree introduced Stoya and then filled her in on the airport explosion that apparently had killed Sergei Markov.

"Are you okay?" she said to Stoya who was managing simultaneously to look fearful and the soul of innocence.

"I am fine," Stoya reported in a small voice. "Thankfully, your husband came along and saved me. But I am afraid the people who blew up Sergei will now come for me."

"Except they probably think you were on that jet," Freddie pointed out.

"Who knows?" said Stoya airily. "I only know I have nothing. I am lost in this world."

"You're not lost, you are here and you're safe," Freddie said. "What you should do right now is call the police."

Stoya reacted in horror. "No police! I cannot speak to the police!"

Naturally, thought Tree. Did he ever encounter anyone who wanted to speak to the police? Including himself? Not in the Florida world in which he had existed for the past two decades.

"Why not?" Freddie was asking.

"Because there are certain things I would have to tell them I cannot tell them," Stoya replied.

"Like what?"

"Those are the things I cannot tell you."

"Then it's going to be kind of difficult to help you" Freddie said impatiently.

"I do not have papers," Stoya said with a sigh. "I am not here legally. Neither was Sergei. We were supposed to fly in, he said, pick up a certain item of value, he said, and then fly out again."

"The item being the Alexandra Tiara."

"Yes, that's what he said."

What happened?"

"I'm not quite certain. Sergei led me to believe he knew the location of this tiara. But then he called your husband and hired him to find his former wife. I don't know why he would do this, and pay so much money."

"Was this when you kissed my husband?" Freddie asked the question in the same way she might ask if Stoya had shaken Tree's hand.

"It was," Stoya answered with a winsome expression. "I am so bad sometimes. And," she added coquettishly, "your husband is a very nice-looking older man."

"It depends on the day," Freddie noted.

"I would please appreciate a drink," Stoya said, less co-quettish, a little more demanding.

"What would you like?" Freddie asked.

"Whiskey. I must settle my nerves. I am very anxious."

"I doubt whiskey will do that," Freddie said. "Besides, we don't have any."

"You don't have whiskey? I thought all Americans drank whiskey."

"Not this American."

"What do you have? Vodka?"

"White wine. I can pour you a glass of chardonnay."

Stoya rearranged her smile into one of benevolent acceptance. "That would be fine."

Freddie disappeared into the kitchen, giving Stoya a chance to unhappily take in her surroundings. "This place is a dump," she said.

"It's a rental," Tree said. "We're moving in less than two weeks."

"Where are you moving?"

"Chicago."

"Maybe you take me with you." Stoya's face was no longer was either innocent or benevolent. It was now the more seductive face of the Stoya about to kiss him and give him fourteen thousand dollars.

"You had better ask my wife."

Stoya grinned. "That might be interesting. Your wife is very lovely."

"Ask me what?" Freddie was back with two long stemmed glasses.

"I thought perhaps you could take me with you to Chicago."

"I think we can come up with a better solution." Freddie handed Stoya one of the glasses.

Stoya took deep gulps. Her eyes watered. "This is not good wine," she said dismissively.

"I'm afraid it's the best I can do," Freddie said.

11

Freddie made up the single bed in the guest room with fresh sheets. Stoya did not like the look of it. But then she gave a helpless shrug, noting that "the beggars cannot be the choosers." She'd had a fair amount of white wine by then, had gnawed without interest on a chicken leg while she described growing up in a town in Georgia before running away from her abusive father at the age of eighteen and arriving in Moscow. "Where I was a very bad girl. But fun. That's where I met Sergei. I would like to say he was a married man who took advantage of a young woman. But then you could question who exactly took the advantage. Men do not take advantage of me, you understand. I take advantage of them. I am a very strong person."

Except her strength and confidence had suffered with the loss of Sergei and his plane. Stoya had been cast adrift, stranded. The airs she had put on—the sneer taking in the condo's gloomy worn-out décor, the single bed with its lumpy mattress—failed to mask the depth of the predicament she now found herself in. "I have no clothes," Stoya moaned as Freddie handed her a pair of her pajamas. "Never in my life have I been without clothes! What is to become of me with no clothes?"

Or maybe not so lost, Freddie suggested once she and Tree were alone. She eyed the green tote bag Stoya had left on the floor beside the sofa. They could hear the heavy breathing of deep wine-induced sleep coming from the guest bedroom.

"That's a Bottega Veneta bag," Freddie said admiringly. "You can buy me one of those for around ten thousand dollars."

"I'll add it to my Christmas list," Tree said.

Freddie picked up the bag and plopped it down on the glass-topped coffee table. "Let's take a look inside."

"I don't know," Tree said hesitantly. "Feels like a bit of a betrayal."

"If she's telling us the truth, then yes, I suppose it is. However, if we are somewhat suspicious, I say check the bag."

"You don't believe her?"

"You are the detective," Freddie pointed out.

"I thought I wasn't supposed to be a detective anymore."

"You're back to work. Check the bag."

He saw the handgun as soon as he opened it. A Beretta. He lifted it out gingerly.

"Well, well," said Freddie, her eyes widening. "Our poor, helpless Stoya isn't quite so helpless after all. Is it loaded?"

"It is," said Tree.

He carefully laid the gun on the coffee table before returning to the bag filled with makeup, various brushes and combs, and a black leather Gucci wallet.

"You can buy me one of those for a thousand dollars," stated Freddie as he lifted it out.

"We can pay for it with the money she has in cash," Tree said, opening the wallet and thumbing through the hundred-dollar bills it contained. "Stoya's not quite destitute."

"I have a sneaking suspicion that no matter what happens, Stoya will never be destitute," Freddie said.

"Credit cards in her name," Tree said, inspecting the wallet's sleeves. In addition, there was a United Arab Emirates driver's license, an Emirates identification card, a membership card at Swissôtel Spa & Sport, and another membership card at La Maison de Beauté. "It looks as though she and Sergei had taken up residence in Dubai."

"Welcome all Russian oligarchs who can't visit anywhere else in the world," Freddie said.

He dug into a side pocket and came up with a card that read in a beautifully rendered scroll, Luxury Motor Storage. In slightly smaller print below: Safe. Secure. State-of-the-Art. On the back below the address someone had scrawled Bldg 2 and the numerals 1918 in black ink.

"Is that a clue?" Freddie's question would have fit perfectly into a dinner theatre mystery production.

"It's a card for an auto storage unit in Naples," Tree corrected.

"For cars?"

"Possibly Sergei stores his car there."

"Sergei was here illegally," said Freddie in full investigative mode. "According to you, he was afraid to get off his plane. Why would he store a car in Naples? And even if he did have a car in storage, why would Stoya have this card? She certainly wouldn't have a car here. Would she?"

"Unless my hearing is failing, you're suggesting I drive to Luxury Motor Storage and find out for myself what's in there."

"And do it before Stoya wakes up in the morning," added Freddie.

"It could be a wild-goose chase," Tree suggested.

"Whether I like it or not—and I don't—we're in this. I'll put Stoya's purse back together. You get going."

Tree pointed to the coffee table. "What about the gun?"

"I'll hang onto the gun."

"Then she'll know…"

"Let me handle her," Freddie said with confidence.

On the edge of Naples, the pair of sand-colored two-story

buildings that housed Luxury Motor Storage were bathed in the harsh glow of LED floodlights. Tree used the access code on the back of the card that was in Stoya's purse. The iron entrance gate slid open to a wide passageway. On either side, units faced with gleaming rolling steel bay doors fell away in the distance. The unit Tree was looking for was at the end of building two. He parked the car and went to the pedestrian entry next to the bay door. A keypad was on the wall. He keyed in the same code. The pedestrian door buzzed and then sprang open.

He followed a short corridor into a space illuminated by overhead lights, about twenty-five by fifty-five feet, occupied by a gleaming red Ferrari. Sergei did have a car, after all, Tree reflected. Otherwise, the unit was empty except for the cardboard packing boxes at one end. He went around the car to where the boxes were stacked. There were six of them. He opened the top box. It was full of *Playboy* magazines from the 1980s.

Books about the Russian revolution and Nicholas and Alexandra filled the second box. The third box contained six velvet jewelry boxes in colors ranging from red to purple. He laid the boxes on the hood of the Ferrari. The first two boxes contained very expensive necklaces and bracelets. The third box, its crimson cover faded, contained a tiara encrusted with what looked to Tree like diamonds and pearls.

The Alexandra Tiara?

He stared at it on the Ferrari's hood, not quite believing what he was seeing. Was this the real thing? And if it was, why would Sergei be looking for something he already had? By claiming he didn't have it, his competitors would leave him alone. To bolster his claim, he might even hire an aging private detective, not enthusiastic about looking for anything.

But whatever Sergei intended, it had not worked out well for him.

Tree lifted out the tiara, and then replaced it with a necklace from one of the other boxes. He returned the six jewelry boxes to their original positions. He shut off the lights and then, holding the tiara close to him, went out to his car, aware that he was almost certainly being recorded by an omnipresent CCTV camera. There wasn't a whole lot he could do about that. Sergei was no longer in any position to give him a problem.

Inside the car, he pondered what to do with what he could only imagine was a priceless piece of jewelry. Without a whole lot of options, he decided on the glove compartment. It fit nicely. He started the engine and then turned the car around and headed out. As he approached the gate it slid open to admit a black Lincoln SUV. The Lincoln slowed as it drove past Tree. The driver stared straight ahead.

He wasn't absolutely certain, but the man behind the wheel looked a whole lot like the late Sergei Markov.

12

Tree drove down a side street about a block before turning the car around so that he had a good view of Luxury Motor Storage's front gate. As he sat in darkness, Tree began to be plagued by all-too-familiar second thoughts. Had he been seeing things or was that really Sergei Markov? A brief glimpse was all he got. It could have been anyone.

Keeping an eye on the gate, he phoned Freddie. "I was getting worried," she said.

For an instant, he nearly blurted out that he may have found the Alexandra Tiara, then quickly decided to keep quiet until he was a bit more certain as to what was in the glove compartment. "How are things there?"

"Stoya is still asleep. Did you find anything?"

"A Ferrari and a lot of old Playboy magazines."

"That's all?"

Should he tell an outright lie nearly as well? And what should he say about a possible Sergei sighting. "Yes," he said aloud. Hating to have to lie to his wife. But it was for her own protection, he silently told himself. The less Freddie knew, the safer she was.

"Where are you now?"

"Outside the facility." As he spoke, he saw the main gate begin to slide open. The Lincoln SUV came out onto the street and turned right, away from where he was parked.

"Are you on your way home?"

"Shortly," Tree replied as he started the car. "There's something I have to check first."

"What is it you have to check at this time of the morning?" Freddie's voice was infused with an edge of concern.

"I won't be long," Tree said. "I'll fill you in once I'm home."

"I don't know what you're up to, but be careful."

"I'm always careful."

"No, you're not."

Tree caught up to the Lincoln in time to see it swing onto Tamiami Trail. Traffic was light, easy for Sergei to spot someone following him. Tree's hope was that since he had conspired to convince everyone that he was dead, Sergei would not be keeping an eye out for someone tailing him.

The SUV continued on Tamiami for the next half hour or so, to the point where Tree was growing exhausted and having trouble staying awake. Then suddenly the SUV's taillights disappeared. Tree saw a turnoff to the left, Anchor Rode Drive. He made a sharp turn onto the road. He followed along past a sign declaring this was Bahia Point. A white mega mansion was framed by a big moon against a blue-black sky. He caught a glimpse of the Lincoln SUV as it slowed into a driveway.

Tree moved further along the street before turning around so that he could return to the house. There was another brief glimpse of a shadowy figure leaving the Lincoln. Was Sergei arriving home after a hard day of pretending he was dead? Had he gone to his storage unit to retrieve the tiara only to discover it wasn't there? The night would yield no answers, Tree decided as he accelerated. Not unless he went up and knocked on the door. He wasn't about to do that. Besides, he now had what everyone was after. As he got onto Tamiami Trail heading north, another question struck him suddenly: What the hell was he going to do with it?

No answer for that question either.

A subdued dawn light had broken through the night sky as Tree reached Gulf Harbour. He was so exhausted he could hardly keep his eyes open, desperate to crawl into his bed and get much-needed sleep. He was too old to be up all night. Too old for any of this. But how many times had he told himself that over the years? He had only gotten older—and a lot more tired.

And a lot more fed up with himself.

He couldn't decide what to do with the tiara as he parked the car. Tell Freddie about it? Not a good idea with Stoya present. And she posed yet another problem. Never mind the question of what to do with the tiara. What were they to do with Stoya?

As he got out of the car he saw that the door to their condo was ajar. *Shit!* That was not good. Not good at all. He pushed open the door and hurried up the stairs. The living room was a shambles, the furniture upended and ripped apart, pictures torn off the walls.

He called out loudly, "Freddie!" No answer. He called again. The guest bedroom door had been forced open. There was no sign of Stoya. He reached the master bedroom.

Freddie lay on the floor. Not moving.

13

Everything moved in slow motion. Everything was turned on its head. Nightmare was reality. The young doctor's voice seemed to come in an echo from a long way off. Freddie had suffered a concussion from a blow to the head. She was still unconscious. Was she going to recover? Tree's voice didn't seem to be coming from him. They were doing their best. The young doctor's voice was a noncommittal echo. Tree sat with Freddie holding her hand as she lay pale and wrapped in crisp white sheets, attached to a blur of wires and drips and monitors.

And then there were the police. Two female detectives, both wearing jeans and dark sports jackets, no-nonsense women who ushered Tree into a deserted examination room. Tree was directed to sit. The two detectives hovered over him. The detective named Dallas Grant led off the questioning. "You told the officers at the scene that you arrived home and found your place broken into and your wife unconscious on the floor. Is that what happened?"

Numb with a combination of exhaustion and shock at what she was suggesting, Tree babbled something about loving his wife very much and under no circumstances would he ever hurt her.

Neither detective appeared convinced.

The other detective was called Gina Ruiz, a big woman with expressive dark eyes filled with suspicion, her black hair shot through with gray and pulled back into a ponytail. She asked, "Why do you think people would break into your house and assault your wife?"

"I'm not sure," Tree answered, although he was all-but certain the assailants had broken in looking for Stoya. He wasn't about to tell that to the detectives.

"You told the officers you're a private detective?" Dallas Grant looked even more skeptical.

"That's correct."

"On Sanibel?"

"And Captiva," Tree added. "And the surrounding area."

"The surrounding area." Gina shot her partner a look. "Aren't you a little old for that sort of thing?"

"I've retired," Tree explained, as though that might make it more palatable to be a private detective on Sanibel and Captiva. "In fact, we're moving north in a couple of weeks."

"Moving is very stressful," offered Gina. "Maybe that's why the two of you ended up in a fight."

"I told you, we weren't fighting. I came home and found Freddie unconscious."

"At five o'clock in the morning?" asked Gina.

"Yes," said Tree, realizing immediately how bad that sounded.

"What were you doing out till that hour?"

"This is ridiculous," Tree said, angrily getting to his feet. "I should be with my wife not trying to deal with you two."

The two detectives traded glances. Dallas shrugged. "Okay, Mr. Callister, but as soon as she's able to, we will be talking to your wife."

"I'll be sure to let her know," Tree said. He walked out feeling more dazed than ever.

To his immense relief, he found Freddie awake when he came back onto the ward. He took her hand. "How are you feeling?" he asked.

"Like someone hit me with a baseball bat," Freddie murmured. "Which, come to think of it, is what happened."

"A baseball bat?"

"Something like that. Two men in ski masks. I was in bed asleep when they came in. I didn't get much of a look at them. What about Stoya?"

"Gone," Tree said.

Freddie momentarily closed her eyes. "I'm so sorry."

"There's nothing you could have done."

"Still…" Freddie let the sentence drift off.

"I've been with the police, trying to convince them I didn't beat you up."

"How did that go?"

"Not very well. They were ready to put me in handcuffs."

"Serves you right." Freddie said.

"Two female detectives. They will want to talk to you. You might want to leave out the part about Stoya."

"You don't think we should let the police know that she's missing?"

"I'm not so sure she is. When I was at the storage facility, I saw someone who looked an awful like Sergei Markov."

"You're kidding. Are you sure?"

"I followed him to a house in Naples, but it was late and I didn't really get a good look at him."

"So then what are we going to do?"

"We get you home as soon as possible," Tree said.

"That's a very good idea."

Tree held her hand tighter. "I love you."

"I know you do."

"I feel sick about what's happened. When I saw you lying on the floor, I thought…"

"Those aren't tears I see, are they?"

"No of course not." Tree brushed at his eyes. "A tough-as-nails detective doesn't cry simply because he finds his wife beaten and unconscious on the floor at five o'clock in the morning."

"You are many wonderful things, my love, but thankfully tough as nails isn't one of them."

"That's what you think," Tree said, not very convincingly.

"Come here," Freddie said. "I think I will feel much better if you kiss me."

The kiss made Tree feel a whole lot better.

14

Freddie was going to be fine, the young doctor assured him when Tree showed up at Lee County Healthcare the next morning. Just to be on the safe side, though, they were keeping her for another day. Freddie definitely looked a lot better. Tree found her sitting up, the color back in her cheeks, eating a cup of yogurt. "You look as though you should be in here instead of me," she observed.

"I didn't sleep very well last night," Tree said.

And he hadn't. The Orange Man had returned to his nightmares. Damn the Orange Man! Damn his overactive imagination! Damn the life that kept him awake at night.

"Let's talk about your next move." Freddie's voice cut through his determination to feel sorry for himself.

"My next move is to get you out of here, leave Florida as soon as possible—and then do my best to make sure you're never in danger again."

Freddie's wasn't buying Tree's declarations. "Can I make a suggestion?" she offered in a diplomatic voice.

"Sure. What is it?"

"Find out what's happened to Stoya, ascertain whether Sergei really is alive and get to the bottom of what is going on."

"I thought you didn't want me involved?"

"That was before you got involved—against my better judgment I might add. It was also before I ended up in the hospital. I'm leaving out your ex-wife who started all this.

"Yes, we mustn't forget Judy," Tree said.

"Could Judy have sent those two thugs last night?"

"That's not like her," Tree said. "She usually has more subtle means when it comes to dealing with me."

"She might be desperate enough to change the way she deals with you when it comes to finding that tiara—or dealing with Sergei and his friend Stoya."

"That would mean she somehow knew Stoya was with us," Tree said. "That's hard to imagine."

"Funny, every time I can't imagine Judy doing something—she does it. Why do I suspect it's unwise, as it always has been, to underestimate her?"

"Okay, I've got my marching orders."

"Give me one more kiss and then get out of here."

Kissing Freddie, he reflected, could be the easiest thing he would do all day.

As he drove away from the hospital, Tree convinced himself that he had done the right thing not telling Freddie about the tiara. The less she knew, he told himself, yet again, the less danger she was in. But then why not simply return it to Judy? She had sent him to find the tiara. He had found it. Except he suspected that wouldn't end the mess he had gotten himself into. With the tiara in his possession, he had leverage. Without it, he had nothing.

That was what he convinced himself was the case as he came along Bahia Point and the McMansion where he had last seen the supposedly dead Sergei Markov. Stakeouts in seemingly deserted neighborhoods like this one, a lone car parked at the side of the road with an old guy sitting in the driver's seat hour after hour, tended to draw unwanted attention. Approaching noon, only the buzz of cicadas and the incessant screech of a distant leaf blower broke the silence of the neighborhood. Unable to find an unobtrusive vantage point from which to watch the house, Tree thought to hell with it and parked across the street. He went up the long drive to the front entrance and pressed the doorbell trying not to think about all the people who got shot at Florida front doors all the time.

When he rang a second time, the door opened and Alice, the precocious daughter of the Miami fixer Red Dahlia, stood on the threshold. Her small round face lit with delight. "The man with the tree name," she said happily. Alice wore culottes and a striped T-shirt and her pink Crocs. This morning, she was not holding onto her purse with the gun and the cigarettes inside.

"Hello there, Alice," Tree said. "I'm glad you remember me."

"You made Mother very pissed off." She covered her mouth so that her giggle was muffled. "I shouldn't say that, should I?"

"It's all right," Tree said. "I won't tell anyone. Is your mother home?"

"She's out by the pool. Would you like to see her? I like it when you piss her off."

"I certainly don't want to do that. Is she alone?"

"That awful Russian was here, but he left. He's not nearly as nice as you. Would you like me to show you where the pool is?"

"If you don't mind," Tree said.

He followed Alice as she marched across an impressive great room with a vaulted ceiling and big windows that looked out onto an infinity pool and the Gulf of Mexico. Red Dahlia was on a chaise lounge beside the pool. She wore dark glasses and a white bikini that emphasized her lithe tanned body. When she saw Alice approaching with Tree in tow, she removed her sunglasses. Otherwise, she reacted as though Tree arrived regularly at her poolside.

"Look who I found at the front door, Mother," Alice announced in a pleased voice.

"Yes, I can see that." Dahlia kept the sunglasses off and sat up a bit straighter. She said to Tree, "Have you found it?"

"It depends on what 'it' is," Tree said.

"Alice, why don't you run and get my cigarettes?" Dahlia said to her daughter.

"Mother!" Alice stamped her Croc-clad foot. "You promised me you weren't smoking."

"Alice," Dahlia said sternly. "Don't argue with me. Do as you're told."

"I hate you!" cried Alice.

"I understand that," replied Dahlia calmly. "Now get me my cigarettes."

Alice stomped off. That was the signal for Dahlia to replace her sunglasses and lean back on the lounge. Tree tried not to look as she shifted her legs around. "Where was I?" she asked distractedly.

"You were asking me if I had found it."

"I'm not going to ask how you found *me*."

"Clever detective work," said Tree.

"That, I highly doubt."

"Why don't you tell me what you know about Sergei Markov," Tree suggested.

Dahlia removed her sunglasses. Those big blue eyes reflected the sunlight. "Why would I know anything about him?"

"Maybe because I followed him here."

"Why would you be following him?"

"Could be that he is looking for 'it' too. In addition to being the late Alexei Markov's brother, he is supposed to be dead."

"Fascinating," was all Dahlia said.

"Blown up in his private jet at Naples airport."

"You don't say." Dahlia remained steadfastly noncommittal.

"I wonder if he has 'it.'"

"What would make you wonder that?"

"I followed him here last night from a storage unit that isn't too far away."

"And now you're back looking for him and not expecting to find me here." Her full lips curled seductively.

"You could say that."

"Maybe you're smarter than you look." Dahlia shifted her legs around some more. "This whole private detective thing… perhaps I should be seducing you. A woman in a bikini under the hot Florida sun. Isn't that what happens in those pulp detective novels?"

"But this is real life," Tree retorted. "In real life that doesn't happen."

"I don't know about that." The purr was back in Dahlia's voice.

"Ah, but I do."

Dahlia offered a disappointed pout. "Some detective you turn out to be."

"I hear that a lot," Tree said.

Alice was back holding a pack of cigarettes as though it was a dead, rancid animal she was presenting to her mother.

"Thank you, dear," Dahlia said, taking the cigarettes.

"You're awful," accused Alice.

"I'm your mother," corrected Dahlia. She was sitting up busying herself extracting a cigarette. "Did you bring my lighter?"

When Alice failed to answer, Dahlia looked up sharply at her daughter. "Alice?"

"I don't have your lighter," snapped Alice.

"Dear." Dahlia spoke with feigned sweetness. "Go and get my lighter."

This time Alice did not argue. She turned and stomped off. Dahlia shook her head. "That child."

"She doesn't like you smoking," Tree suggested.

"I'm quitting." Tree gave her a look. "I am," Dahlia maintained without conviction. She leaned over and carefully placed the cigarette on the little round table next to the chaise lounge. Once she had done that, Dahlia rose majestically and closed in on him. Her slim oiled body glistened in the sunlight. "I can't waste any more time with you," she stated archly.

"I know, you've got cigarettes that need smoking."

"Tell me what you're doing here."

"A couple of men broke into the place my wife and I are renting. They assaulted my wife and put her in the hospital. In all likelihood, they were looking for the tiara."

"I don't know anything about that," Dahlia said.

"Sergei's girlfriend was with us. Now she's missing."

"You're not suggesting I had anything to do with it, are you?"

"Did you?"

"Don't be ridiculous," Dahlia said dismissively. "Honestly, you're starting to bore me, Mr. Tree Callister." To demonstrate her boredom, Dahlia replaced her sunglasses.

"Maybe this won't bore you," Tree said. "When I followed Sergei here last night, he had come from the storage unit where he, possibly in partnership with you, was hiding the tiara. Did he tell you it was missing?"

"Supposing for a minute any of what you just said is true, how would you know about it?"

"Let's leave it that I do know."

Dahlia removed her sunglasses so that she could look at him with something approaching respect. "Is it possible I might have underestimated you?"

"Anything is possible."

"Don't tell me that somehow you have the tiara."

"Supposing I do?"

She drew closer. He could feel the heat coming off her. "That deal we discussed."

"We didn't discuss any deal."

"You and me." She made it sound as though she was promising to be with Tree forever.

"What about Sergei."

"Sergei is dead. Don't worry about him."

"His ghost must have driven to your place last night."

"You're seeing things." Dahlia tried to sound convincing. She didn't do a very good job of it. She leaned forward and tried to kiss him. He turned in time so that her lips brushed his cheek.

"I'm too old," Tree said.

"Not if you've got the tiara."

"Mother!" Alice had returned, marching across the pool deck. Dahlia backed away. "What are you doing?"

"Did you bring my lighter?"

"I couldn't find it," Alice announced with satisfaction.

"Damnit!" Dahlia exploded in exasperation. She swung around to Tree. "See what I have to put up with?"

"Mother!" called out Alice, stamping her foot. "Don't talk to Mr. Tree like that."

"This is to be continued," Dahlia snapped at Tree.

"I came here looking for Sergei—and answers," Tree said.

"I don't have either. But *if* you have the tiara—or you *know* where it is—and don't tell me, well, let's say it's won't go well for you, Tree goddamn Callister. It won't go well at all."

Dahlia swept away across the deck toward the house.

Alice sadly watched Dahlia disappear. "I don't know about Mother," she lamented. "I think it has to do with her smoking." Her face intense, Alice dropped her voice to a conspiratorial whisper. "Don't listen to Mother. That awful Sergei is alive. He was here last night." Her voice dropped further, to the point where he could barely hear her. "I think they are *sleeping* together."

She raised and lowered her eyebrows dramatically before turning to hurry into the house after her mother.

15

Home from the hospital, Freddie was still weak but all business. No, she didn't want tea. Whatever would make Tree think she wanted tea? She didn't particularly like tea. And no, she wasn't hungry. Maybe a glass of chardonnay a bit later.

"In the meantime," Freddie went on, maintaining her businesslike tone, "I want you to tell me what so far you haven't told me."

"About what?" asked Tree. As though he didn't know.

"About what happened after you left me the other night."

"What makes you think anything happened?"

"I know you, Tree," Freddie stated with certainty. "You're withholding something. It's not the first time. Tell me what it is."

With an acquiescent sigh, Tree told her about going to the storage locker and finding the tiara. "Wait a minute," Freddie interrupted. "You found the Alexandra Tiara—the priceless Alexandra Tiara—in a box in a storage garage."

"That's right."

"Where's the tiara now?"

"It's in the glove compartment of the Mercedes."

"The Alexandra Tiara is in the *glove* compartment?" Freddie's voice filled with disbelief. She was shaking her head, never a good sign, Tree thought, when his wife was contemplating the extent of his insanity.

"I didn't know what else to do with it," Tree explained.

"God, Tree." Was all she could say. Still shaking her head.

"There's something else."

"I hate it when you say that," Freddie said with a groan.

"I told you about seeing Sergei Markov as I left the storage facility."

"Yes, you did, which probably means he knows the tiara is gone."

Tree nodded. "I told you I followed him to a house at Bahia Point. I went back this morning. Sergei wasn't there but Red Dahlia and her daughter were."

Freddie didn't seem particularly upset. "Did Dahlia kiss you?"

"She offered to partner with me," Tree said. "She purred when she made the offer."

"She strikes me as the type who would purr," observed Freddie. "Does she know you have the tiara?"

"She doesn't know for sure, but she suspects, which is why she made the offer."

"But you didn't tell her."

"No."

"Have you told anyone else? Judy for instance?"

"No one knows except you."

"What are you going to do? Tell Judy?"

"I don't know. I haven't gotten that far."

"Well, you'd better hurry up and get there," admonished Freddie. "I don't think I can take many more beatings."

"I should never have agreed to meet Judy in the first place. I should have listened to you."

"There are endless numbers of times over the years when you should have listened to me," Freddie noted wearily. "But it's a little late for regrets. We have no choice but to deal with this tiara—and I think we have some responsibility for what's happened to Stoya."

"You said you didn't get a good look at the two men who broke in."

"That's right. As I told you and the police, they were wearing ski masks. I can understand them breaking in here, thinking we might have the tiara," Freddie said. "But why would they take Stoya?"

"Maybe they think Sergei has the tiara—and until last night they would be right—hoping to trade Stoya for the tiara."

"Would Sergei have made a deal like that?" Freddie asked.

"Who knows?"

"Sergei might not, but you would." Freddie looked at him pointedly.

"I would?"

"It gets Stoya back and gets us off the hook with the tiara."

"What about Judy?"

"Judy lied to you and put both of us at risk and landed me in the hospital. It's up to us to get out of the mess she created the best way we can.

"In the meantime," Freddie went on, "I will take you up on that glass of chardonnay you're offering."

"I wasn't offering you a glass of chardonnay."

"I could have sworn," Freddie said.

"I love you," Tree said, suddenly overwhelmed by this incredible woman. Even after so many years together, he still couldn't believe he had been lucky enough to marry her.

"I'll love you more once you get me the chardonnay," Freddie said, her arms around his neck, beginning to kiss him."

"This is distracting me from the chardonnay," observed Tree.

"Good," said Freddie breathlessly. "I have now decided there are other activities I have in mind."

"What other activities might they be?"

"Come with me into the bedroom and I will show you," Freddie said.

They went into the bedroom. The chardonnay was forgotten.

The ringing telephone woke Tree from a sound sleep. He was determined to ignore it until Freddie shifted around and said, "Answer it..."

"It's probably Judy," Tree said. "I don't want to talk to her."

"Talk to her," Freddie ordered sleepily.

Tree picked up the phone.

It wasn't Judy.

"Don't hang up," a raspy male voice ordered.

"Who is this?" Tree responded.

"Someone who knows where Stoya is."

"Where is she?"

"You get Stoya in exchange for the tiara."

"Supposing I don't have it."

"Then don't show up tomorrow afternoon. Two o'clock. The mermaids. The Weeki Wachee Springs State Park."

The phone clicked loudly in Tree's ear.

16

By the time Tree awoke the following morning, Freddie already had been out to the car and retrieved the Alexandra Tiara from the glove compartment. It lay on the desk beside the laptop she was busily working on.

"There are in fact mermaids on the Weeki Wachee," she announced, as though this were the best possible news. "The Weeki Wachee Springs features a mermaids show. It's quite famous."

"With real mermaids?" Tree was trying to shake himself awake, steeling himself for whatever hell the day would bring. Including mermaids.

"Women dressed as mermaids," Freddie corrected.

"That's disappointing. I was hoping for real mermaids."

"They are underwater, apparently, so pretty close to the real thing."

"I don't know about you going up there," Tree said.

"Is this the part where you tell me that I can't go because it's too dangerous?"

"No, this is the part where I tell you it's too dangerous for either one of us. Besides, you've just been released from the hospital."

"Right. The part where you tell me I need rest."

"You need rest."

"There you go. But I'm fine. Besides, I feel somehow responsible for Stoya," Freddie said. "Plus, I don't want to miss the famous mermaid show."

"I don't know," Tree said hesitantly. "We go up there, what are we walking into?"

"A three-hour drive and we will find out," Freddie said with a reasonableness that Tree was not sharing. "We'll be on time for the mermaids."

"This is the part where I say I can't believe you want to do this," Tree said.

"That's usually my line," Freddie said.

The northbound I-75 interstate transported Freddie and Tree to a much different Florida; a darkly lush gothic landscape of thick pine forests, magnolia and bay trees, more varied and complex than the flat blandness of the southwest coastal regions. If bad things happened in bright sunlight further south, here they took place in the shadows, dripping with humidity, better hiding places for the greed and lust that were everywhere in the state but somehow were more at home up here.

Perhaps because the tourists had yet to return in their pre-Covid, pre-hurricane numbers, Tree and Freddie reached the Weeki Wachee Springs State Park in plenty of time for the two o'clock mermaids show. "Let's leave the tiara in the glove compartment for now," Freddie suggested as Tree parked. "I'm not at all sure about this."

"That's two of us," Tree said.

Inside the park's four-hundred-seat auditorium, families crowded along benches facing a series of big windows through which the limestone face of the spring's deep caves was a watery blue-green dreamscape amid swirling bubbles erupting from strategically placed air hoses.

"A former naval officer created the first shows in 1947," reported Freddie, reading from the screen on her phone. "He was the one who developed the idea of using air hoses so the mermaids could breathe underwater. He started in an eighteen-seat theater, then expanded it in 1959."

She continued reading. "The mermaids can't see underwater because they pack their eyes with dry-eye ointment that allows them to keep their eyes open."

Tree craned around to see if anyone in the audience might be—what? Slightly mysterious, would help. Except no one in the crowd looked even vaguely mysterious. "I'm not even sure what we're looking for," Tree said aloud.

"Someone in a trench coat with beady eyes who hasn't shaved for a while," Freddie suggested, putting her phone away.

"As far as I can see, no one here fits that description," Tree said.

The loudspeaker system came to life and an announcer said the show was about to begin. The theater darkened, the audience settled and the scene on the other side of the windows brightened to reveal gracefully swirling and diving mermaids equipped with impressive tails, every so often taking a breath from their dangling air hoses. "Those tails have to be specially manufactured," Freddi whispered to Tree. "Each tail costs over three thousand dollars."

The expensively tailed mermaids performed an underwater version of Hans Christian Andersen's *The Little Mermaid*. A mermaid surrenders to a sea witch in order to obtain legs. Naturally, she is saved by a handsome prince who defeats the witch. Tree couldn't help but compare the handsome prince's battle to his own fight. He too had to overcome forces of evil. Except as the show ended, the audience vigorously applauding, those evil forces had not shown up.

Wearing the only unhappy faces, Freddie and Tree joined the crowd exiting the theatre. Gladys Demchuk fell into step beside them and said, "What about it, you two. Did you enjoy the show?"

17

The glare of bright sunshine made Gladys look drawn and old. She had put on weight since Tree had last seen her escaping in her pickup truck away from a hurricane and a murder charge. Today she wore jeans and a T-shirt, her russet hair pulled back in a ponytail. "You haven't answered my question," she said to Tree.

"I think we both enjoyed the show," Tree replied in a level voice. "What about you, Gladys?"

"I missed most of it, just came in at the end. A happy ending. I like that. Those mermaids are something else."

"What are you doing here, Gladys?" Freddie demanded, doing a remarkable job of not looking totally gobsmacked.

"Why don't we go over to one of the picnic tables in the park so we can talk," Gladys suggested.

"Why should we do that, Gladys?" Freddie didn't move.

"I know this isn't what you're expecting," Gladys said reasonably. "But please listen to what I have to say."

"To put it mildly," stated Freddie, not so reasonably.

"I think you'll find it worthwhile to hear me out."

Freddie and Tree exchanged uncertain glances. Then Tree made a resigned hand gesture. "Why not?"

They followed Gladys along a stone path into a wooded area where a picnic table stood in the shade. Tree hesitated before sitting down. "Are you alone?" he asked.

"Just me, Tree," Gladys said seating herself. "Not to worry."

"Where you are concerned, Gladys, I worry." Nonetheless, Tree eased himself onto the bench. Freddie followed.

"They sent me because we know one another."

"Do we Gladys?" Tree said. "I don't know you nearly as well as I thought I did."

"Give me a break, Tree, you knew me well enough to make use of my nasty side when it suited your purposes. When it didn't, suddenly I'm a stranger."

"Let's say I didn't know you were a killer," Tree said.

"Yeah, you did," Gladys said with certainty.

"Who sent you?" Freddie asked.

"After I left you—"

"After you ran away," Tree interjected.

"Sure," acknowledged Gladys. "If that's the way you want it, I ran, disappeared. I found myself in some curious places meeting some interesting people who introduced me to other interesting people. I ended up in Vienna being interviewed by an organization looking for someone like myself—the person you say you don't know, Tree, but in fact, you do."

"Go on," Freddie urged.

"They said they could provide the cover I needed to keep me out of prison. I liked that idea, needless to say, and so after a good deal of back and forth, I became part of them."

"What is this organization?"

"They don't like it when their name gets mentioned, and the name won't mean anything to you, anyway. They are off the grid, operating in a gray area, doing things that others can't do, finding what others can't find."

"Like the Alexandra Tiara," Freddie ventured.

"That's an item we are tasked with retrieving," Gladys said.

"Was it your people who broke into our condo and beat up Freddie?" Tree demanded.

"It was an overreaction," Gladys said. "I wasn't part of it."

"But you do have Stoya," Freddie put in.

"Do you really have the item we are looking for?"

"You don't sound convinced," Tree said.

"With you, Tree, I never know quite what to expect, particularly when your ex-wife Judy Markov is involved. Let's say I wasn't expecting you to end up with it."

"We wouldn't be here if we didn't have it." Freddie spoke in her impressive let's-get-down-to-business voice. "Do you have Stoya or not."

"We will turn this woman over to you once I have the tiara."

"That's not going to work," Tree said. "We give up the tiara when we have Stoya."

"As I said, they sent me because you know you can trust me."

"I don't know that," Freddie said. "Just the opposite, in fact."

Gladys gave Freddie a hard look. "Look, my role is to act as the go-between, to smooth the way forward so to speak. You've already had an unpleasant experience with these people. You know just how nasty they can be when it comes to getting what they want. I want to make sure there is no repeat of that."

"And what is the way forward?" demanded Freddie.

"You bring the tiara to the address I am about to give you," Gladys said. "I will meet you there. Don't worry, it's not far."

"Why can't we do things right here?" Freddie asked pointedly.

"This isn't the place for making exchanges," Gladys stated. "We'll all be more comfortable at this address. My people can be assured that you are alone, that you haven't brought police with you." She dropped a card with an address printed on it. She got up from the table. "I will expect you in an hour."

Gladys walked off across the park. Tree wanted to call after her. But call after her and say what?

He couldn't think of anything and then it was too late. Gladys had disappeared into the crowd gathering for the next show.

A two-story house stood above the green, calm Weeki Wachee River. Tree parked the car on the gravel driveway. The driveway was otherwise empty. Freddie said aloud what Tree was thinking: "Where's Gladys? I don't like the look of this."

"Leave the tiara in the car," Tree said.

The house loomed in front of them, silent in the heat of the day. At the entrance, Tree knocked a couple of times. "I don't think anyone's here," Freddie said tensely.

"Let's try the back," Tree said. "Maybe someone's there."

They went around to a yard that sloped down to a dock. On the river, two kayaks appeared, their occupants fighting the current. Perhaps, thought Tree, the Weeki Wachee was not quite as peaceful as it appeared. Maybe the house wasn't either.

Tree crossed an inlaid brick terrace to a sliding screen door. "Hello? Gladys? Are you here?" he called through the screen. There was no response. He tried the screen. It slid open easily. He stepped into a sitting room. Freddie crowded behind him. "This isn't right," she whispered.

"Hello? Gladys, if you're here, answer me," he called again.

There was no response.

"Wait here," Tree said to Freddie.

"Be careful," Freddie said, the universal warning issued when someone was about to be anything but careful.

Tree stepped forward and then paused. Did he hear something? He turned to Freddie. She nodded slightly, alert.

From somewhere deep in the house, they heard a low groan.

Tree went out of the sitting room and made his way into

a hallway. The body of a man lay by a narrow staircase. "My God, Tree," he heard Freddie say from behind him. He heard another groan from upstairs. Louder this time. "Better stay here," Tree said to Freddie. He started up the stairs.

There was a second body at the top of the stairs. Nearby, Gladys was sprawled on the floor. The front of her T-shirt was soaked in blood from multiple gunshot wounds. She was chalk white as Tree knelt to her. Behind him, he could hear Freddie arrive with a horrified gasp.

"Freddie, call 911," Tree said, taking Gladys's hand.

Gladys moved her head back and forth as though to signal it was too late for that. "Sorry, Tree...screwed up badly..."

"What happened, Gladys? Who did this?"

"Everyone wants it...do anything..."

"Who? Gladys? Tell me who these people are."

Behind him, he could hear Freddie breathless and anxious on the cell phone to 911.

Her mouth opened, trying to form words. "It's..."

Tree bent closer. "What is it, Gladys?"

Gladys said something he couldn't quite make out."

"Gladys? What are you trying to say?"

"Volkova..."

Then she stopped moving her head. Her eyes went blank.

"Oh, God." With the phone in her hand, Freddie fell to her knees beside Tree. "Oh, God...no!"

Her phone emitted the scratchy voice of the 911 operator demanding to know their location.

18

Freddie and Tree were all-too familiar with the chaotic scene that soon unfolded. The arriving police and emergency workers, the ambulances, the firetrucks, the police vehicles, a competing discordance of sirens and flashing lights. The detectives were from the Hernando County Sheriff's Office, two middle-aged men with crewcuts, dressed in identical short-sleeved white shirts and loosened ties. They gave every indication they had been around the block many times.

Freddie was in tears, Tree close, both of them stunned. At the same time, long experience kicked in: Say as little as possible about how they came to be present at what was obviously a murder scene—a scene where three people had been killed, and where there was no sign of Stoya, the missing woman who was the reason for them being there. They were not about to tell the police that part of it.

Sanchez had jet black hair and was the taller of the two detectives. Dowd was squat, with a lot of gray running through his thinning scalp. They were polite enough but obviously suspicious of a couple that had little idea where they were, discovering three dead bodies in an otherwise empty house.

Freddie and Tree sat on the patio under the watchful eyes of stunned neighbors gathered to witness the spectacle of a murder scene. The shaky story Tree told was that they had driven from Fort Myers to see the mermaid show at Weeki Wachee State Park. While there, they had run into Gladys Demchuk, who used to work for Tree when he was operating his Sanibel Sunset Detective Agency. She had invited them back to her house for coffee. When they arrived, they found one man on the ground floor, another upstairs—and Gladys. There was no one else in the house.

"Except we don't think this is Ms. Demchuk's house," Detective Dowd said.

"We didn't know," Freddie said.

"You have no idea why the deceased would have asked you to come here?" Sanchez had stopped writing in the notebook on his lap.

"We didn't think about it," Tree said. "We just assumed this is where Gladys was staying."

"This place is a rental, you know, Airbnb shit." Dowd wasn't taking notes. He kept his small dark eyes on the two of them as if at any moment they might make a run for it. "Ms. Demchuk didn't give you any idea why she was here with two men?"

"We were going to get caught up this afternoon," said Freddie. She used a tissue to dry her eyes.

"I understand this must be traumatizing but do you have any idea who might have done this?"

"Like we've told you, we weren't expecting to run into her at the park," Freddie answered truthfully. "So no."

Sanchez and Dowd traded quick glances. Tree couldn't tell if the detectives were buying any of this. Probably not, since it was the job of police not to easily believe most of what they were told.

Finally, the two detectives ran out of questions to ask and accordingly there were no more lies to tell. The detectives seemed reluctant to let them go, perhaps sensing there was something missing here, a piece of the puzzle Freddie and Tree were holding onto.

It was growing dark by the time they were allowed to get back to their car and start south toward home. "I feel terribly, awfully sick," said Freddie, slumped in the passenger seat.

"I wouldn't have thought anything could kill Gladys," Tree said glumly. "I guess I was wrong."

Freddie opened the glove compartment. "Just making sure it's still there," she said.

It was.

"Gladys getting killed over this ugly thing." She regarded the tiara with something like disgust. "I'm tempted to throw it into the Weeki Wachee River."

Freddie heaved a sigh and closed the lid. "God knows what's happened to Stoya."

"Assuming that Stoya was even there," Tree said.

"You think she might not have been?"

"Why would someone kill three people and not kill Stoya?"

"Why would anyone kill Gladys when she didn't have the tiara?"

"Someone who thought she did," Tree replied. "She managed to say a name before she died. Volkova. Maybe this Volkova killed her and the others thinking the tiara was there and then discovered it wasn't."

Freddie cast a glance at Tree. "You know what I'm thinking? If we're looking for answers we are going in the wrong direction. They are back where we just came from."

"What do you want to do?"

"What do *you* want to do?" Freddie threw the question back at him.

"What are we going to do if we go back?"

"Finding out about someone named Volkova might be a good start," Freddie suggested.

Tree glanced in the rearview mirror. One moment there was nothing on the roadway behind him. The next, bright headlights flashed in his rear-view mirror.

"Now what's this guy up to?" The light from the vehicle filled the interior of the car.

Tree had a moment to squint against the intense light and notice Freddie beginning to turn to try to see what was coming behind them before there was a loud crash and a tremendous jolt. The car veered wildly, Tree fighting to keep control of the wheel. A mass of trees came at him. There was a loud whomp when the car struck the trees. Tree heard Freddie's cry of alarm. The windshield shattered and folded in on him.

His seatbelt locked. Airbags exploded open. He lost consciousness.

19

"Now you've done it," sneered the Orange Man. He wore a dark blue suit and a red tie, his orange hair was arranged impeccably as he walked around inspecting the crumpled remains of the Mercedes. "Now you've killed your wife."

"No!" Tree cried in a panicked voice. "No, that's not possible. Freddie's fine."

"Look at the car. It's totaled." The Orange Man jabbed a chubby finger at the hood which was twisted back, exposing the engine. "Do you really think anyone could have survived that?"

"I know Freddie's fine," Tree protested.

"She's dead, you fool," the Orange Man scoffed. "You killed her with your carelessness, stumbling into messes that you have no idea how to get out of."

"She never wanted me to do this," Tree moaned. "I didn't listen to her. My ego always got in the way. I wish I could go back, do it all differently."

"Well, it's too late now," said the Orange Man. "There's no going back. You've killed the love of your miserable life and now you're going to die too. That's what losers do, they not only get themselves killed, but they take the people they love with them."

"I want to go back—I want to make it up to her," Tree cried. "Please, give me another chance—one more chance!'

"Hey! Hey! Take it easy there, pal."

Tree opened his eyes to find a bald heavyset man in green hospital fatigues leaning over him. His expression was a mixture of amusement and concern. "Sounds like you were having a real bad dream."

"My wife," Tree said, struggling to sit up. "Where's my wife?"

"Don't know anything about a wife," the nurse said. "You've been in an accident and from what I've heard, you're lucky to still be with us."

"Where am I?"

"Oak Hill Hospital in Weeki Wachee."

"My wife," Tree said again. "I'm worried about my wife."

"Look, I'm a nurse here, name's Nikolai, just making sure you're all right. The doctor will be in soon to have a look at you. He can answer any of your questions."

"This is crazy," Tree said angrily. "My wife's got to be here. I want to see her."

"You've had a rough time," Nikolai said sympathetically. "Give me a few minutes and I'll see what I can find out about your wife."

"I would appreciate that," Tree said, settling somewhat.

"Can I get you anything?"

"Water would be great," Tree said, realizing how dry his mouth was.

"Coming up," said Nikolai. He was back in a moment with a plastic cup. He helped Tree sit up so that he could gulp down the water.

"That's better," Tree said.

They were interrupted by the arrival of Detective Sanchez. An unhappy detective from the look of him, Tree surmised. Sanchez said to Nikolai, "I'd like to have a word with Mr. Callister in private."

"Sure thing." With a quick nod Nikolai ducked out of the room.

Sanchez advanced to Tree's bedside. He looked down at him without showing any particular sympathy. "How you doing, Tree?" Not much more sympathetic.

Interesting how police officers who disliked him and longed to put him behind bars, always addressed him by his first name, like old buddies getting together for a friendly chat.

"I'm worried about my wife," Tree responded. "Do you know if she's here in the hospital?"

"Your wife?" Sanchez looked puzzled. "What about her?"

"She was in the car with me. Someone rammed us from behind."

"From what I understand, you were alone in the car," Sanchez said mildly.

"That's crazy," Tree said. "Freddie was in the car with me. This happened after we left you. Just down the road. Where else would she have been?"

"Look, obviously I met your wife this afternoon at a murder scene, under suspicious circumstances that we are still investigating," Sanchez said. "But I have no information as to what happened to her after we released the two of you."

"I don't believe this," said Tree with a groan.

"The report I looked at before coming over here was that you were alone in the vehicle that appeared to have been rear-ended by a hit-and-run driver," Sanchez said.

"Where's my car now?"

"I assume a towing company took it into Weeki Wachee. But believe me, you won't be driving that baby again. It's a write-off."

"I have to find my wife." Tree tried to swing his legs out of the bed, only to be stopped by the racking pain.

"I understand you broke a couple of ribs," Sanchez said indifferently.

"Now you tell me," Tree grunted, easing himself back down.

"Listen, I'll check into your wife's whereabouts as soon as we're done here. But I've got some questions that may or may not relate to what's happened to your wife."

"She was with me in the car...I don't understand," Tree said forlornly.

"When my partner and I spoke to you, you seem to have left out a few pertinent details about Gladys Demchuk."

"I don't know what you mean," said Tree. His mind was in a fog. All he could think about was Freddie and what could have happened to her.

"You failed to mention the fact that Ms. Demchuk was previously known as Blue Streak, an adult performer in Los Angeles. She has been on the run, wanted in connection with the murder of the actor John Twist on Sanibel Island."

Tree didn't say anything.

"You have previously been questioned extensively in connection with her disappearance, there being suspicion that you may have helped her get away."

"I didn't do anything to help Gladys."

"Did you not think any of what I just told you might have been relevant to our investigation of Ms. Demchuk's murder?"

"I guess we were so upset finding Gladys dead..." Tree allowed his voice to trail off. He was desperate to get this over with so that he could deal with Freddie's disappearance, the rising horror of not knowing if his wife was alive or dead.

"A wanted fugitive involved in a high-profile murder case—and you *accidentally* run into her at a mermaid show in Weeki Wachee?"

"That's what happened," Tree said. Again, more or less true.

"Come on, fella, don't give me this shit. This woman was

accused of murder. Now she has been murdered. If what you say is true, your wife also is missing. Tell me what's going on here."

"I wish I knew," Tree said—which was true enough and he hadn't even told Sanchez about Stoya, also missing, and the Alexandra Tiara that everyone seemed to be after. Thinking about this made him more anxious than ever to get out of here.

"Please, Detective Sanchez," begged Tree, desperation in his voice. "Can you help me find my wife? Issue a missing persons bulletin, anything you can do."

"Sure, I can, Tree. I want to help you. Freddie seemed like a sweet gal. I would hate to think anything bad has happened to her. But if I help you, I need you to help me. Am I making myself clear?"

"What would you like to know?"

"I asked you before, but let's try it again: Who could have killed Gladys? What is it that you're holding back from me?"

"Excuse me, but what's going on here?" A youthful man with curly black hair wearing glasses with brown frames stood on the threshold.

"Detective Sanchez from the Hernando Sheriff's Office," Sanchez announced. "I'm conducting an interview with Mr. Callister."

"Well, I'm Dr. Travers of the hospital." Dr. Travers marched authoritatively into the room. "I don't care who you are or what you're doing, I don't want you doing it. Not until this man has recovered a whole lot more than he has up to now."

Sanchez let out a sigh. "Okay, we're just about finished here anyway." He raised an eyebrow at Tree. "Unless you have something more to tell me."

"Please, just find my wife."

"Give some thought to what I need from you," Sanchez

said. "Meanwhile, I will do what I can to try to find out what's happened to Ms. Stayner."

"I appreciate that," Tree said.

Sanchez laid a card on the table beside Tree's bed. "That's my number. I expect to hear from you." He gave the doctor a curt nod on his way out.

"I'm sorry about that," Travers said. "If I'd known he was here, I would have booted him out sooner."

"It's all right," Tree said. "I'm hoping he can find out what's happened to my wife."

"Yes, I understand you've told the nurses that your wife was in the car with you."

"That's right," Tree said.

"I had a chance to speak to the paramedics who brought you in. They say that you were the only person in the car when they arrived."

"This is impossible," Tree said despondently. "Freddie was right there in the car with me."

"I'm sure the authorities are on it," the doctor said, becoming businesslike. "In the meantime, you have issues that require attention."

"I need to get out of here," Tree said.

"You're suffering a couple of bruised ribs, a possible mild concussion. We stopped some internal bleeding when they brought you in here. We need to do some more tests to make sure it stays that way. Also, a scan to make sure that brain of yours is functioning properly."

"If it was functioning properly, I wouldn't be here," Tree said.

"But you are here," replied the doctor. "Let's get you better so you can find your wife."

Tree was too tired to argue. He was nearly asleep, sensing

Dr. Travers had slipped away. He told himself that he had to stay awake, stay sharp, find Freddie.

Somehow.

Movement from somewhere in the room pulled him out of his somnolent state. Coming from the shadows, it took Tree a moment to recognize Nikolai. He held a syringe. *What's he doing with that syringe?* Tree wondered sleepily.

"It's all good, Mr. Callister," Nikolai said softly. "It'll be over in a moment."

Over? What would be over? Tree's brain was trying to work through this as Nikolai reached his bed.

Why was the nurse now concentrating intently on directing the syringe at his IV drip? In bad movies, he would be administering something that would kill him.

But this wasn't a bad movie. This was real life. Nikolai loomed over him, his face somber.

"Don't do it!" Tree's alternative voice broke through the fog surrounding his brain. Then another voice, not his own, issued firm instructions: "Back away from him—now!"

Tree struggled to clear his head, to peer through the shadows of his mind. In the dim light, he had to be seeing things. That could not possibly be Judy Markov holding a nasty-looking pistol to the side of Nikolai's head. Nikolai appeared unnerved, frozen in place. "Drop the syringe," Judy ordered.

"What are you doing, lady?" Nikolai asked in a strained voice.

"Getting ready to blow your brains out if you don't do what I say," Judy retorted.

"You wouldn't do that lady," Nikolai said with far too much confidence.

"Sure I would," Judy said.

Nikolai hesitated and then dropped the syringe. Judy

chanced a glance at Tree. "Can you get out of bed, Tree?"

"I...think so," Tree said.

"I want you to very carefully take his IV drip out," Judy said to Nikolai.

"I can't do that," Nikolai said.

"One of two things. Three things, actually. Either you do as I say or I march you out to reception and we call the cops to report a nurse trying to kill one of this hospital's patients. Or, and this is the one I prefer, I just shoot you and get it over with. I'll plead 'stand your ground'. This is Florida so even if it comes to that, no jury would ever convict me."

Wordlessly, Nikolai bent to remove the IV drip.

Once that was done, Judy said, "Now we are going over to the wheelchair beside the door."

Tree managed to struggle into a sitting position as Judy, keeping her gun against Nikolai's head, guided him to the door. He was back a moment later pushing the wheelchair. Tree, his head clearer, lifted his legs off the bed, braced himself against the mattress so that he could lower himself into the chair.

"How are you doing?" asked Judy. "Are you going to be okay getting out of here?"

"Let's go," gulped Tree, although moving anywhere was the last thing he wanted to do. Still, if the alternative was getting killed...

Judy addressed Nikolai: "Now what we will do, we will wheel your patient out to the parking lot. No big deal. Just in case, I will be following with my trusty gun at the ready. Do you understand?"

Nikolai nodded.

"Okay," Judy said. "Let's move."

As Judy had orchestrated it, the scene for anyone who took any notice was a nurse wheeling his patient through a hospital, quiet at this time of night. The difference was the gun Judy held against Nikolai's ribs.

Once they were outside, Judy announced, "That's fine, I can take over from here."

Nikolai drew the wheelchair to a stop. The night air was cool. It helped to further revive Tree. He watched as Nikolai stood back while Judy faced him with the gun. "I don't suppose you'd care to tell me who put you up to this."

"Don't know what you're talking about," Nikolai said sullenly.

"If I had more time, I would make sure you know what I'm talking about. But this is your lucky night. You didn't kill anyone and you didn't get killed. Now get the hell out of here."

Nikolai gave Tree a sideways glance. "You take care of yourself, Mr. Callister. You're okay tonight thanks to her." He nodded at Judy. "But don't kid yourself. You're in a lot of shit."

"Is it Volkova?" Tree asked.

Nikola's eyes widened, the only indication that the name meant anything to him. "I've said enough."

"Beat it," Judy ordered. "Make sure you tell your people that you screwed up."

Nikolai lowered his head and slumped away.

"What are you doing, Judy?" Tree asked as she started to push him towards the parking lot.

"What do you think I'm doing? As usual, I'm saving your ass."

20

From where he was lying in the rear of her SUV, Tree could make out the outline of Judy's head as she drove fast through a black night. Fighting to hang onto consciousness, aching everywhere, Tree had no idea where they were going or what his ex-wife might do with him. Nikolai, his would-be assassin, was right. He was in a lot of shit.

"That guy back there, Nikolai." Tree croaked, barely able to get the words out. "Did this Volkova put him up to it?"

"Don't worry about Volkova," Judy said.

"Then you know who he is."

Judy didn't say anything.

Tree managed to work himself into a sitting position so that he had a view of Judy in profile. She was captured in the glow of the kind of dashboard he imagined would be found in the cockpit of a 747.

"Judy," he repeated.

"This is the height of irony, don't you think? Your former wife saving your current wife."

"Gladys Demchuk is dead."

"I know that," Judy said.

"Before she died, she mentioned the name Volkova. Who is he?"

"He was my Russian liaison at the Kremlin. A powerful man."

"A killer?"

Judy didn't answer.

"Judy, talk to me."

"I'm trying to drive the goddamn car," she said heatedly. "We will get some answers in Sarasota."

"Sarasota? What's in Sarasota?"

"It is where a lot of stupid, dangerous people with ridiculous, dangerous ideas are headquartered."

"Who are these stupid people with dangerous ideas?"

"They believe they are patriotic Americans, waving the flag and announcing they are for freedom, but it's all bullshit. They are led by a former high school teacher who calls himself Orcus, Alexander Orcus. He and his people support my former friend Vladimir. Like everyone else looking for the tiara, he believes it will solidify his relationship with the beloved president."

"And they have Freddie?"

"Orcus thinks you have what he wants." Judy said this as though only a fool could think otherwise. "He can get us to Freddie. But we must put our hands on the tiara."

Tree didn't say anything.

"Tree," Judy said after a time. "You met with Gladys Demchuk in Weeki Wachee. I know she's been working for dangerous people. I have to assume you somehow have the tiara—or Gladys *thought* you have it. I'm not sure what you and Freddie were thinking meeting with Gladys, a loose cannon at the best of times, but that meeting probably got her killed."

"We were trying to help free Stoya."

"Gladys was killed because she went off the reservation. She probably thought she could get the tiara from you and then sell it to the highest bidder. Big mistake on her part."

"What about Stoya?"

"I doubt Gladys even had her," Judy said. "You don't need to worry about Stoya. She's fine."

"How do you know?"

"Because women like Stoya are always fine. It's only fools

like you who think you can save them. They don't need saving."

"What happens if I do have the tiara?"

"Do you?" Judy's voice coming from the front had grown tense.

"What happens?"

For a time, there was only the sound of the car rushing against the night. "Tell me," Judy said finally.

"I know where it is," Tree allowed.

"If we have what everyone wants," Judy stated, "then it's going to make it a whole lot easier to get your wife back."

When Tree didn't answer, Judy snarled, "Tree, quit screwing with me. Do you have it or not?"

"Let's get to Sarasota, let's get some of the answers you're talking about."

"You bastard," Judy said. "You had better have it."

Yes, Tree thought. It would be a whole lot better if he had it.

Except he didn't.

Tree must have fallen asleep for the next thing he knew Judy was driving through what looked like the outskirts of Sarasota. "There you are," Judy said, as Tree groaned in pain as he lifted himself up.

"How long have I been asleep?" he asked.

"Quite a while. You needed the rest. How are you feeling?"

"There's a drummer banging loudly against my head and my ribs are on fire, but otherwise I'm fine. How about you?"

"Driving through the night with my ex-husband, how could it be any better? Like old times."

"I don't remember us driving through the Florida night."

"That's right, I could never get you to go on vacation."

"That's not true," Tree said.

"Your selective memory—something else about you that's like old times."

"It was all a long time ago," Tree said gently.

"Three wives ago. Curious how some wounds never heal."

"I've apologized many times—tried to make it up to you by getting involved in your various schemes, like now."

"We're getting close," Judy said by way of shutting down more talk of Tree's attempts to make amends—attempts Judy had never bought into. They passed the John Ringling Museum grounds on North Tamiami Trail. Not far from the museum, Judy swung the car into a parking lot past a sign welcoming them to Golden Sunset Resort.

Tree looked at Judy. "What is this?"

"Quit asking so many questions," Judy responded irritably.

A paved parking area was enclosed on three sides by a two-story motel complex. Judy came to a stop and turned off the engine. "Follow me," she said. She was out of the car before Tree could object.

"Shit," he said opening the passenger door. It was when he tried to get out that he discovered he was going to have a lot of trouble. Judy saw him struggling and helped him lift his legs onto the pavement and then braced him so that he could rise to his feet. "The invalid Tree," she said. "I like it."

"I can only imagine," Tree said through gritted teeth.

He leaned against the car to gather his strength and then hobbled behind Judy as she made her way toward the motel. The blue door at Room 12 opened.

Red Dahlia said, "I'm dying here. I don't suppose either of you has a cigarette."

21

I thought you quit smoking," Judy said, pushing past Dahlia.

"You sound just like my daughter." With the hint of a smirk, she turned to Tree. "What happened you?"

"It's a long story," Tree said.

"I hear it took your ex-wife to save your life." Dahlia's smirk widened.

"The story of my life," Tree said.

"But not before you got the shit kicked out of you," Dahlia said.

"Where's Alice?" Tree asked.

"She's with her good-for-nothing father so I can take care of all this shit."

"Curious, I was sure you weren't exactly on Judy's side," Tree said following her into the room. Dahlia's clothes were spread out everywhere. Two suitcases were open on one of the beds.

"Let's say the sides have gotten kind of wobbly."

"She was blinded by the amount of money I'm paying her," Judy said, glancing around the room.

"I guess you didn't have enough left over for decent accommodation," Dahlia said dryly.

"They've got Tree's wife." Tree wondered if that was Judy's way of changing the subject away from the substandard accommodation.

"I'm sorry to hear that, but who has the goddamn tiara?" Dahlia said.

Judy pointed at Tree. "Our dear friend here says he knows where it is."

"As I suspected." Dahlia regarded him speculatively. "You're looking more attractive all the time, Tree." That seductive purr was back.

Judy waved a dismissive hand. "Let's concentrate on what happens next. Have you heard from the General?"

"He's agreed to meet us this evening."

"Where?"

"Where else? The Hollow."

"The General?" Tree gave Judy a puzzled look. "Who's the general? I thought we were after this Orcus?"

Dahlia arched an eyebrow. "You told him about Orcus?"

Judy made another unconcerned gesture. "He's got to know sooner or later."

"I don't know…" Dalia's voice trailed off into uncertainty.

"I thought we had to get to Orcus," Tree said. He had slumped into a nearby chair. Everything in his body was hurting.

"The General can get us to Orcus," Judy said.

"Major General Buck Ares," explained Dahlia. "He leads Legio Three."

"What is Legio Three?"

"Very hush-hush," said Dahlia. "Very secretive. Legio Three is as close as Buck is ever going to get to what he thinks is a private army. He is Orcus's puppet."

"How do you know all this?" Tree asked.

"Because," Dahlia said, "I used to work for the General."

"Don't forget the part where you slept with him," Judy added cattily.

"I slept with him on… *occasion*."

"Which is why Dahlia, who, incidentally, is a former CIA agent—"

"Very former," Dahlia interjected.

"Which is why the General dumped her," Judy finished.

"He did not *dump* me, as you are so fond of saying." Dahlia made an unpleasant face. "Buck is an asshole, what can I tell you."

"But he is still willing to see you," Tree prompted.

"I think he wants you back," Judy said.

"He doesn't want me," Dahlia corrected. "And I certainly don't want him. He wants that tiara."

"Let me get this straight." Tree leaned forward in his chair. "This Buck Ares doesn't have Freddie, but he can get us to this other guy named Orcus who does."

"I'm hoping we won't have to go to Orcus." The nervousness was back in Dahlia's voice. "I'm hoping Buck can settle this."

"Let's find out," Judy said noncommittally.

"You keep saying that," Tree said glumly.

"Only because it's true."

"Make a note of that," said Dahlia. "Judy speaking the truth. It doesn't happen very often, believe me."

Judy ignored the jibe. "Do you have a key for Tree?"

Dahlia threw Tree a room key. He was too weak to catch it. Dahlia shook her head. "Boy, you're going to be a great asset, aren't you?"

Judy bent to retrieve the key and handed it to him. "Get some sleep. I'll wake you up in a few hours. Hold out your hand."

"What?"

"Do as I say, Tree. Hold out your hand."

As soon as he did, she dropped a tablet onto his palm.

"A painkiller," Judy said. "Take it. Otherwise, you're never going to get through this."

He closed a fist over the tablet. "Where are you going to be?"

"Don't worry, I won't try to sleep with you."

"If you hear a knock on the door, it'll be me," Dahlia said with a certain amount of coquettishness.

Judy aimed a warning glance in her direction.

"Only kidding," Dahlia said. She gave Tree a wink.

Entering his room, it was all Tree could do to stagger as far as the bed and flop down. He felt terrible. His body ached, his head throbbed. He was having difficulty processing what he was hearing. A general named Buck Ares. A private army, Legio Three. Ares wasn't holding Freddie. It was the mysterious figure known as Orcus. But Ares could lead them to Orcus—and Freddie. Was any of it true? Could he even begin to trust either Judy, the manipulative oligarch fallen on hard times, or Dalhia, the former CIA agent who apparently changed allegiances as casually as she changed clothes?

He could ponder all he wanted, the reality was he had little choice but to go along with these two women, hoping against hope that it would get Freddie back. Once she was safe, they would leave this place and never come back. They would live quietly and Tree would never again place Freddie in danger.

Ever!

He forced himself off the bed, feeling so dizzy he had to lean against the wall for support so that he could strip off his clothes. He swallowed the painkilling tablet Judy had given him. He stood for an eternity under the hot spray of the shower. That made him feel somewhat better. Staggering back into the room, he fell onto the bed, never even managed to get under the covers before he fell into a deep sleep.

Thinking of Freddie. Dreaming of Freddie. Praying for Freddie…

22

When he awoke several hours later, Tree dressed and then made his way to room twelve. He found Dalhia alone, seated at a desk by the window, jamming rounds into a magazine intended for the Glock lying nearby. "This gun is a bitch to load," she grumbled. It's okay at the beginning but by the time I shove the seventeenth round into the magazine my thumb is killing me."

"What's the gun for?" Tree inquired.

"In case I have to shoot someone," Dahlia answered, shoving the magazine into the Glock's stock. "I won't be able to do that if I don't load the gun."

"Are you planning to shoot someone?"

"I'm not thinking about it. But I've discovered it's better to be safe than sorry. Feeling any better?"

"A little less tired," Tree said. "Where is Judy?"

"She's bringing the car around. We leave in a few minutes."

"To do what?"

"I believe a chat with the General is on the agenda."

"Will he help?"

"Better if we had the tiara." She raised an eyebrow at him. "You *do* have the tiara?"

"I don't have it with me but I know where it is."

The doubtful eyebrow raised higher. "I'm not sure that's going to be enough."

"You know him," Tree said. "What do you think?"

"Where the general is concerned, I never know what to think." She got up from the table and went to her handbag with the loaded Glock. She was placing it inside when Judy arrived.

"How are you feeling?" she asked Tree.

"A little better," Tree offered.

"He still looks like shit, and he can barely walk," Dalhia said, eyeing Tree but talking as if he wasn't there. "Is he going to be a liability?"

"We need Tree with us," Judy said. "He'll be fine."

Would he? News to Tree. Still, he thought he'd better say something. "I will be okay," he claimed in a voice that sounded more like a lie than a reassuring declaration. "There's no way I won't be part of this, if there's any chance of getting to Freddie."

"Let's stop arguing and get going," Judy ordered in the tone she adopted when she didn't want an argument.

"Off we go," agreed Dahlia. As though they might be on their way to dinner.

The Hollow turned out to be only a few minutes away. A lush garden outlined in spotlights obscured a wide concrete tunnel, black painted and decorated with illuminated quotations like "To disarm people is the best and most effectual way to enslave them." Not a line from Martin Luther King, Tree guessed. The tunnel gave way to a deserted light-splashed patio area.

Judy and Dahlia traded glances. "Okay," breathed Dahlia. She had become edgy as she stared around the patio.

Presently, a tall man emerged into view, startling Tree and the two women. "Jesus, Buck," Dahlia breathed. "You scared me."

"I can't imagine scaring you, Dahlia," drawled the tall man with an insouciant grin. "Or you, Judy."

"Not scared, Buck," Judy said, "just extra careful whenever you appear unexpectedly."

The General's hair was cropped short and spiked with gray. His jaw might have been carved out of granite. Men with jaws like that are enlisted automatically, Tree speculated, no questions asked. His blue eyes sparkled with a zealot's fervor. If anyone had ever been built for battle, it was Major General Buck Ares. He was dressed not in battle fatigues, but a white Polo shirt and casual light brown slacks. The American warrior might have recently come off the golf course.

His zealot's eyes landed on Tree. "And this must be the much talked-about Tremain Callister. The curiously named Tree. The Tree in search of his wife."

"That's why I'm here," Tree acknowledged.

The General focused on Judy. "I assume the Tree man has brought us something in exchange for his wife."

"Tree doesn't have the tiara with him," Judy explained mildly. "But he knows where it is and can obtain it quickly when necessary."

That drew a frown from the General. "That is not what we agreed," he said tersely.

"Is Freddie here?" Tree interrupted. "I want to see her."

"Like you, Tree man, I don't have what you're looking for, but I can obtain it, when necessary," Ares said.

"The tiara is in Sarasota. I will tell you where as soon as I have Freddie."

"That's not good enough," Ares pronounced. "Come back when you have what you say you have."

"Enough bullshit, Buck." Dahlia's face had hardened. "Do you have his wife or not?"

"This is not the time to make me angry, Dahlia." Ares's eyes glinted dangerously, a look similar to the one Tree imagined he adopted when sending his troops into battle.

"Tell us where the woman is," Dahlia demanded. "If you don't have her, tell us who does. Orcus? Is that who has her?"

"I don't like it when you say that name," Ares said with a frown. "That name is irrelevant."

"Is it?" Dahlia moved closer to Ares. "I don't think it is. Orcus pulls your strings, Buck. The wizard in your Oz. Where is he? Where's the woman?"

"Our meeting is over. Get out of here, the three of you. Don't come back unless you have something."

Tree marvelled at how fast Dahlia got her Glock out and pointed at Ares.

"You must be joking," he said quietly.

"You know me, Buck," Dahlia said. "I never joke with a gun in my hand."

"You're not going to shoot me, Dahlia," Ares said confidently.

"You always underestimate me, Buck," Dahlia said a moment before she shot him in the leg.

Buck grunted loudly and crumpled to the flagstone floor. "Bitch!"

"God, Dahlia…" Judy's breath was coming in short bursts.

Dahlia stood over the writhing General. "The next round goes into your other leg, Buck. Where is the woman?"

"Jesus, Dahlia," Ares groaned between clenched teeth. "What the hell are you doing?"

"Doing something I should have done a long time ago, you shit. Answer me, where's the woman?"

"The other room, Jesus."

Tree bolted to the exit at the rear of the patio and into a narrow passageway, calling Freddie's name. A response came from behind a door at the end of the passage. He tried the

latch. Locked! Desperately, he kicked at the door. In his weakened state, his kick had no effect on the door All it did was send
a vast amount of pain shooting up his leg.

Then, with a click, the door opened. Stoya stared at Tree in
amazement. "Was that a gunshot I just heard?" she asked.

23

What are you doing here?" Stoya asked, peering at Tree in mystification. For someone who supposedly had been abducted, he thought she looked pretty darned good.

"You were supposed to be kidnapped," Tree said. "We've been trying to find you."

"I *was* kidnapped," she maintained. "Strange, nasty people brought me here—to my new friend, Buck."

"Why did you lock the door?" demanded Tree.

"So I have some privacy away from weird people spouting their silly nonsense. It is too much. I take a pill. Everything is much better—except for that noise. Was it a gunshot? These people are crazy. They are shooting guns!"

"We've been looking all over for you," Tree said.

"For your information, I do not need to be found. I am in very good hands, thank you very much."

"With the people who kidnapped you?"

"As it happens, yes," Stoya conceded. "Sergei was no good for me. My new friend Buck—a general in the American army, you should know—he knows how to treat me properly." She frowned. "Incidentally, where is Buck?"

Judy poked her head in the door. "He's in the other room," she said.

"Please tell him I must see him immediately. I cannot stand to be here."

"I think you'd better go to him."

"Why?"

"He's been shot."

"*Shot*?" gasped Stoya uncomprehendingly. "Why would he be *shot*?"

"He wasn't cooperative." Judy said it in such a way as to suggest anyone who was not cooperative could end up shot.

Stoya cried out as she shot past Tree and out of the room, shouting, "Bucky!"

Judy and Tree traded looks: *Bucky*? They followed Stoya back to where Bucky writhed and gasped on the floor, overseen by Dahlia, the offending gun still in her hand, keeping her eye disdainfully on the General.

Stoya's face filled with horror. She cried out and then fell melodramatically upon her true love. She cradled Ares in her arms and glared angrily at Dahlia. "Bitch," she exploded. "How could you?"

"It was easy," reported Dahlia. "I simply thought of my time with him. The trigger practically pulled itself."

Tree bent to the groaning Ares. "I ask you again. Where is she? Where is my wife?"

"Go to hell."

Enraged, Tree seized Ares by the shirtfront and drew him up so that his face was close to the General's. "*Where* is she?"

Ares just smirked. "I'm not telling you shit."

Tree swung around to Dahlia. "Give me your gun."

"Hey, take it easy," Judy said in a warning voice.

"No, let's see what Tree is made of," Dahlia said. She handed him her Glock. "It'll save me the trouble of shooting him again."

Tree, holding onto Ares, jammed the Glock into his mouth. Stoya screamed in alarm. "Leave him alone!"

Tree wasn't listening. "You bastard," he yelled. "This is my wife. This is someone I love." He jammed the gun harder into

Ares's mouth. "Talk to me!"

"And Buck," Dahlia interjected, "Tree is basically a nice guy. Nice guys aren't usually wandering around shooting horse's asses like yourself. If he can't follow through, I'll be only too happy to take over and finish the job for him."

Ares made desperate gurgling sounds. "Don't know," he sputtered as soon as Tree removed the barrel.

"I know you're too dumb to be let out on your own," Dahlia said, leaning beside Tree. "Then who? Who is behind all this shit? Orcus? Tell me it's Orcus."

"Someone you shouldn't mess with if you know what's good for you," Ares breathed.

"Let's dispense with the meaningless threats," Dahlia said. "How do we get to Orcus?"

"You don't want to go near Orcus." Ares was having trouble breathing as he spoke. "Orcus will do anything that gets him what he wants, and he wants that tiara."

"Does he have my wife?" demanded Tree.

"All I know, I don't have her, okay? And don't ask me where Orcus is, because I don't know. No one knows. That's why he's Orcus. If he has your wife, he will be in touch—God, I'm starting to lose it...". He was bleeding across the floor. His face had turned a chalky white. "I need a doctor..."

"Bucky!" Stoya howled. She looked up imploringly at the others. "Please, he's going to die! He needs help."

Tree rose and handed back Dahlia her gun. "Thanks," he said.

"What do you think?" Dahlia pointed the gun at Ares. "Should we shoot him, anyway?"

"No!" cried Stoya. She threw herself protectively across Ares's body.

"We should get him to a hospital," Tree said.

"No! No hospital!" Ares had become as panicked as his new girlfriend. "Jesus, that'll bring the police."

"Good," said Dahlia. "Let's leave him to bleed out. The world will be a better place without him, believe me."

With Stoya weeping loudly in the background, a debate ensued as to what to do. It was agreed that calling an ambulance would involve the police and a lot of questions that no one present wanted to answer. It was finally decided that Stoya, once they got her settled, should call a doctor who was part of Ares's organization and therefore could be counted on to keep quiet.

"It would be easier to just shoot him," Dahlia opined. "Put him out of his misery."

"Let's rein in our worst impulses," Judy put in.

"Oh, I don't know why we should do that," responded Dahlia.

Somewhat reassured that Dahlia would not shoot him again, Ares called her a bitch. Dahlia responded by kicking his wounded leg. She looked entirely satisfied as Ares screamed in pain.

"What would your daughter think?" Judy shot Dahlia a hostile glance as she drove south towards Fort Myers.

"Alice wouldn't think anything because she doesn't know anything," said Dahlia, curled against the passenger's-side door. "Besides, I wasn't really going to shoot the bastard more than once. I was hoping Tree would do it for me."

"A woman scorned," said Judy.

"Not that any of it did much good," Tree said. "Freddie is still missing, and I'm getting really scared." He paused before adding, "I'm going to the police."

"Orcus probably has the police taken care of around these parts," Judy said. "They're not going to be much help."

"Who is this guy, anyway, that everyone seems to be so scared of?"

"Orcus isn't his real name, of course," Judy explained. "Orcus is the Roman god of the underworld. That's how he fancies himself. His real name is Damian Fargo. The Fargos are a wealthy and therefore powerful family in this state. Damian or, as he prefers to be known, Orcus, is not so much the family's bad seed as he is the worst among a bunch of bad seeds. The family patriarch, Nestor Fargo, made his fortune in the 1980s in for-profit hospice care. Orcus's step-mother Alina is rumored to have control of the family fortune, but she generally listens to her stepson and does what he wants."

"Which is what?" tree asked.

"He funds people like that lunatic Buck Ares. His idea of making America great again. He loves Vlady, thinks he is the kind of strong man needed to run things here. He would do just about anything for Vlady."

"Says the woman who until recently was up to her neck with Putin's bunch," interjected Dahlia.

"Listen to who's talking." Judy shot her a glance in the rearview mirror.

"Merely a gun for hire," Dahlia said defensively.

"Let me try to understand what's happened here," Tree interjected. "Judy, you acquired the Alexandra Tiara years ago."

"Not me, Alexei," Judy corrected. "He had it when we married, like I told you before. Back then it was no big deal—or so I thought. Alexei kept it in a drawer in his office. He didn't even bother to lock the drawer."

"Then you inherited it when Alexei died."

"That's right, like I inherited everything else. The tiara was the least of my concerns—until the rumors of war in Ukraine started. That's when the chill began to set in from Moscow. I got the sense Valdy's people were distancing themselves from me. Then out of the blue, a message came, demanding the return of the tiara. I wasn't about to hand it over given the icy climate—not without a few concessions."

"Which they didn't want to give you, I'm guessing," Tree said.

"Let's say the negotiations had been ongoing when the hurricane hit. Thankfully, I wasn't in town at the time. What Ian didn't destroy, the subsequent fire did."

"But you held onto that tiara because without it you had no leverage with your pal, Vlady, is that it?"

"Judy is not exactly Vlady's pal at this point," put in Dahlia.

"Is that where you and Alice came into the picture?" Tree asked.

"Buck Ares phoned me in Miami," Dahlia explained. "A simple job, he said. Pick up this tiara. A five-thousand-dollar payday for retrieving it from a burned-out house and then driving it up to Sarasota."

"But it wasn't there because somehow Sergei Markov got there first," Tree said.

"All I know is that it wasn't there," Dahlia said.

"But you somehow found it, Tree." Judy gave Tree what looked like an accusatory glance. "You and Freddie. Which is undoubtedly why Freddie is missing."

"Why we're trying to keep you alive and find Freddie," Dahlia added.

"That's what we're going to do," Judy proclaimed. "We're going to get her back."

"But Tree," Dahlia said pointedly, her gaze steadfastly on him. "When we do, you had better be able to deliver the goods."

24

It was after midnight by the time they turned off the Daniels Parkway exit to Fort Myers. Tree was exhausted, feeling very weak and still in a great deal of pain. He desperately wanted sleep. Later, he would figure out what to do next. Right now, he had no idea beyond vague thoughts of somehow getting to someone named Orcus, who suddenly loomed large in his life.

Where did all these strange people come from? he wondered as Judy slowed along McGregor Boulevard. What had he unleashed simply by driving to Judy's burned-out shell of a house? He should never have allowed himself to be talked into it. He was torn between wanting to strangle Judy and his need for her help if he was ever going to get Freddie back.

"Now what?" Judy asked once she pulled up in front of the Gulf Harbour gate.

"We have to go back to Weeki Wachee," Tree said.

Tree could hear Dahlia exhale loudly in the back. Judy said simply, "You could have saved a lot of time by telling us that earlier."

"I'm telling you now," Tree said.

"Better late than never," Dahlia opined.

"Get some sleep," Judy advised. "You look terrible. I'll pick you up in the morning and we'll drive back up there."

That sounded too simple, thought Tree. But it was something. What else was there? He had to trust Judy, despite a history that suggested trusting Judy was not a good idea. He looked at her. She seemed to read his mind. "You can trust me," she said, and then added nastily, "Besides, you don't have any choice."

Trusting Judy. Right. Tree nodded noncommittally. "I'll see you tomorrow."

He got out of the car and watched her drive away. Feeling uneasy. Had he given too much away by revealing he at least knew where the tiara was?

Coming along the roadway, he managed to convince himself that he retained at least some control. The tiara afforded him the leverage he would need to negotiate Freddie's return. Around him, good people were all sound asleep, unconcerned about kidnapped wives or missing tiaras or people out to commit murder. What a nice life that must be, Tree reflected, once again beating himself up for not listening to Freddie for making the quiet life around him an impossibility.

Feeling sorrier for himself than ever, Tree reached the entrance to his condo and fished in his pocket for the key. For a moment he panicked that somewhere along the way, the key had been lost, but no, he still had it, inserted it into the lock and opened the door.

A business envelope that had been pushed through the mail slot, lay on the floor. He picked it up. The Sarasota company that had towed his car had sent the bill. Somehow, Four Palms Towing had found his address. He carried the envelope up the stairs. Sergei Markov was seated in one of the lime-green recliners that Freddie hated. He said, "There you are Mr. Tree Callister. I thought you were never going to come back."

Tree, recovering from the surprise of seeing him, placed the envelope on the table.

Sergei said, "Do you not want to ask me how it is that I'm not dead?"

"I can see you're alive," Tree said taking a deep calming breath. "What I don't understand is what you are doing here."

"In my rather desperate need for a safe hiding place after

they blew up my jet, I thought of you. Particularly since I believe it was you who stole my tiara."

"I didn't know it was yours," Tree said.

"You stole it from me. That suggests that it belongs to me," he argued.

"I don't have it." Tree reminded himself that there was actually some truth to what he was saying. He moved further into the room, so tired and aching that it was all he could do to keep standing.

"Then you must know where it is," retorted Sergei. He was sitting up now, not quite so relaxed.

"What I don't understand is why you hired me in the first place. You already had what everyone wants."

"Perhaps a miscalculation on my part," Sergei admitted regretfully. "If Judy knew I had the tiara, it could have created problems for me. However, if she thought I was in search of it like everyone else, that I had even gone so far as to hire her ex-husband, a local private detective, not known for any expertise in these matters…" He let the sentence drift off. He punctuated it with a shrug. "However, I was not expecting you to be quite as effective as you turned out to be. So here I am in your place, seeking the tiara."

"Everyone wants it," Tree observed.

"But not everyone has a gun they are willing to use to shoot you," Sergei said. Sure enough, Tree saw that he somehow had added a gun to his right hand.

"You might be surprised," Tree said. "Or maybe you wouldn't." He added, "I don't care about a tiara. I need it so I can get my wife back."

"Your wife, not a good situation," he said, actually sounding somewhat sympathetic. "Tell me where is the tiara and perhaps I can help you."

"Everyone says that, but my wife is still missing."

"Do you have any idea who could have taken her?"

"I keep hearing about a man named Orcus."

Sergei's eyes lit up. "Ah, yes, the great and feared Orcus. The man who blew up my plane."

"Are you sure about that?"

"As sure as I am about anything where that bloody tiara is concerned. I assume that if Orcus has your wife, he would return her in exchange for the tiara."

"Something like that, except I don't know how to get in touch with him."

"He hasn't contacted you?"

"Not as yet."

Sergei furrowed his brow. "Unusual." Then he brightened even more. "But you see my friend, this is where I can be of help. I can contact Orcus."

"Even though he blew up your plane, presumably trying to kill you," Tree pointed out.

"That only means I know him all too well." Sergei leaned forward intently, the gun more or less forgotten in his hand. "You and me, my friend. With the tiara, we reach out to the Orcus. We get your wife back."

"But then Orcus has the tiara, not you."

"Let me worry about that," Sergei said. "We get the tiara. We get your wife. I will take care of the rest."

Tree didn't know what to think. His mind was a blank. He could barely keep his eyes open let alone decide if Sergei was for real. Suspecting there was no one he could trust—or should trust.

"Listen, I've been in a car accident, I've had to go to hospital. Right now, more than anything else, I need sleep."

"I understand," Sergei acknowledged. "My friend, you look like shit, if you don't mind my saying."

"Funnily enough, everyone tells me the same thing," Tree admitted. "It may have something to do with the fact that I feel like shit."

"Then you must get some rest. I will remain out here, making certain necessary arrangements—and ensure that you do not, as they say, take off."

Yet again Tree was faced with the reality that he didn't have a choice. He was about to drop from exhaustion and Sergei, as friendly as he had suddenly become, continued to make sure his gun was in full view.

"Sure," Tree said wearily.

That got a big smile from Sergei. A triumphant smile? Tree wondered.

He was too tired to worry about it.

The Orange Man was naked.

He lay on his back atop a vast canopied bed, his great belly rising and falling. He didn't appear to notice Tree. What was he doing in the Orange Man's bedroom? The heavy drapes covering the windows were the color of gold as was the thick carpeting. The oil painting in a gilt frame covering most of a wall showed the Orange Man astride a great golden horse.

The bedroom door opened and Freddie, wearing a golden silk robe, entered the room.

"Freddie," Tree called to her. "What are you doing?"

Instead of answering, she slid into bed and embraced the Orange Man. He kissed her. As he did, Freddie's eyes fixed on Tree. "What did you expect?" she said pulling away slightly from the Orange Man. "You got me into trouble. You wouldn't listen to me. Now you can't find me. I've decided to stay with a real man, a man who knows how to take care of me."

"I told you," the Orange Man said to Freddie. "He's a loser. A woman like you deserves so much better than this guy."

"I'm afraid you're right," Freddie murmured. "I've given him all sorts of chances over the years. I told him I wanted to leave and go back to Chicago. He wouldn't listen and now it's too late."

"You'll love my place in Florida," the Orange Man said.

"You don't have any lime-green recliners, do you?"

"Are you kidding?" said the Orange Man disdainfully. "Baby, I live in gold."

"I love gold," Freddie murmured. She kissed him again, more passionately this time.

"Please, Freddie," Tree begged. "Please give me another chance. I will make this right, I promise. Somehow, I will find you and make this right."

The Orange Man and Freddie weren't paying any attention.

"Freddie, please," Tree pleaded. "Listen to me…"

The Orange Man stopped kissing Freddie long enough to sneer at Tree. "Get lost, loser. Your wife's where she should be. She's with a winner."

"No," Tree cried. "No, no, no…!"

"Tree, Jesus, Tree," a voice called out.

Tree opened his eyes. Judy Markov leaned over him. "What's the matter with you?"

It took him a moment to realize there was no Orange Man and Freddie was not with him. He was in the bedroom of his condo, a worried Judy backing away as he sat up. Behind her, Dahlia wore an amused expression. "It looks like our Tree was having a bad dream."

"Where is he?" Tree asked.

"Where is who?" Judy traded looks with Dahlia.

"Sergei Markov. He was here when I went to sleep. Where is he?"

"What are you talking about?" Judy said. "There was no one here when I came in. Just you, bellowing like a lunatic."

Tree went out to the kitchen where he had left the envelope he had picked up when he came in. It was torn open. The bill for having his car towed to Weeki Wachee lay beside it. "Shit," he said.

"What?" Judy demanded.

"Sergei, he knows where the tiara is."

25

A lice I'm not kidding," Dahlia was saying into her cell phone. She was in the front seat as Judy sped north back to Weeki Wachee. Tree was slumped in his usual position in the back, his head throbbing, still feeling lousy.

"Mother is working today so I can't be with you. Therefore, you must do what Maria tells you to do. You are not the boss, no matter what you think." Dahlia paused to listen, irritated. "Young lady, you are to do as you are told or there is no Puerto Vallarta for you at March break. I will take another little girl who behaves properly and does not sass back." Another pause. "You don't think so? Just try me, young lady."

"Honestly, that child," Dahlia announced after she rang off. "I'm at my wit's end with her."

"Maybe she needs to spend more time with her mother," Judy said.

"The perfect mother speaks," Dahlia said snidely.

"Talk to that guy in the backseat," Judy said grimly.

Instead, to Tree's relief, Dahlia began to rummage in her bag. Judy delivered a series of suspicious sideways glances. "Are you looking for a gun or a cigarette?" she asked.

"Supposing I said gun?"

"That's fine," Judy said. "But no smoking in the car."

Dahlia looked unhappy as she tossed her bag aside. "What I don't understand is how anyone could be dumb enough to tell Sergei Markov anything, let alone the location of the tiara."

"He found the bill from the towing company and probably put two and two together."

"You're a fool," Dahlia said as though his foolishness was beyond dispute.

"My brother-in-law is a failed oligarch, desperate to do anything to get back into Vlady's good graces," Judy said. "He was lying to you. How could you ever believe he could get you to Orcus when in all likelihood, it was Orcus who tried to kill him."

"He said that wouldn't be a problem."

"He played you, Tree," Dahlia said with satisfaction.

"Now he's got a head start on us." Judy was shaking her head as she drove. "Honestly, Tree, I don't know what you were thinking."

"I was thinking I want my wife back, and I will do anything to make that happen," Tree retorted.

"I keep telling you, we will get her back, but we need that tiara."

A tiara in exchange for the woman he loved, thought Tree. The world had come to this.

The day had turned blistering hot by the time they finally found Four Palms Towing outside Weeki Wachee, the yard to which the ruined Mercedes had been hauled. A couple of big tow trucks were parked in front of a rundown garage off the highway. The garage faced a sea of broken and rusting vehicles, a graveyard hiding evidence of the carnage on Florida highways behind a clapboard fence.

An unshaven kid in the ramshackle office was much more interested in what was on the screen of his phone than he was with three intruders—until he got a look at Dahlia. She brought him to attention. He actually put his phone aside.

"What's with that Mercedes anyway?" asked the kid in a lazy drawl. "Fella's been here earlier looking for it."

"What kind of fellow?" demanded Tree.

"Foreign fella," reported the youth. "Funny accent. Not sure what happened to him."

"Did he go out to the car?"

"Not sure what he did. I was real busy on the phone."

"Can you direct us to the car?" said Judy impatiently.

"Like I told that other fella, it's out there somewheres. I have a hard time keeping track of everything that comes in here. Computer's been down for a couple of days. Can't be too far away, though. Other fella got me to look it up."

"How did he do that? Didn't he have to identify himself?"

"He did, sure," said the unshaven kid confidently. "Gave me his name. Tree Callister. Matched the name in our records."

"I thought your computer was down," said Dahlia.

"They are, but we been taking new entries manually."

"I'm Tree Callister, not the other guy."

"You are?"

"I am."

The unshaven kid looked at Tree blankly. "How was I supposed to know that?"

"So where is the car?"

The kid shrugged and waved a disinterested hand in the direction of the yard. "Somewheres."

By the time they went into the yard, the unshaven kid was already back on his phone. They searched through ranks of tangled wrecks stacked to allow for narrow lanes that meandered through the yard. When Tree finally located the Mercedes three-quarters of an hour later, he was amazed that he and Freddie had survived. The force of the collision had shredded the rear and pushed the remnants into the back seat. As he came closer, a sickly odor hit him. "What the hell is that?" Judy asked, wrinkling her nose.

Tree knew that smell and wished he didn't.

The passenger door of the Mercedes was open. Tree could see the body slumped forward against the dashboard. Sergei Markov's face was turned toward him, his eyes wide, perhaps reflecting the disbelief of an oligarch who missed getting killed once, but could not dodge death a second time in a sunblasted Florida junk yard.

Judy appeared, holding her nose, expressionless as she stared at the body of her brother-in-law.

"Is this worth it?" Tree demanded angrily.

"Where did you leave the tiara?" was Judy's response.

"If it's still there, it's in the glove compartment." Tree glared at Judy. "You're going to have to move him. This is so important to you? Move him."

Judy hesitated. Dahlia pushed past her. "Oh, for God's sake." She leaned into the car, shoving at Sergei so that he fell sideways, giving her access to the glove box. She pressed the latch and the lid sprang open. The owner's manual was inside.

But no tiara.

"Shit," said Dahlia.

Judy looked grim, but said nothing as Dahlia shut the glove box and straightened. "Let's get out of here."

"We should call the police," Tree said.

"Are you out of your mind?" Dahlia flared. "Call the police and we'll never hear the end of it. Let that kid in the office deal with it."

Judy nodded. "Dahlia's right."

"The kid saw us. He can identify me. This is my car."

"Right now, that doesn't matter," Judy said. "You want to get Freddie back, we get out of here."

"But we don't have the tiara," Tree said.

Dahlia pointed to Sergei's body. "I'm willing to bet Orcus

did this. He's got the tiara and he's got Freddie. We get to him and it's one-stop shopping as long as we don't waste time with the police."

Judy cast a final glance at the dead Sergei. "I never liked the bastard," she said quietly. "Still..."

Leaving the sentence unfinished, she turned and marched away back through the yard, Tree and Dahlia following.

In the parking area, the unshaven kid leaned against Judy's car, an insouciant smirk firmly in place; the snotty kind, Tree thought, indicating the kid knew something that they didn't and was feeling pretty smug about it.

"Find what you're looking for?" he asked, folding his arms.

"What do you suppose we were looking for?" Tree asked.

"For one thing, I guess you found the car."

"No, we didn't," Judy said quickly. "This place is too big. We decided it's not worth the trouble."

"Is that right?" The kid didn't move.

Tree spoke up. "Why do you ask?"

The kid shrugged. "I dunno. There might be something you're looking for that has nothing to do with a car. You might be looking for something else."

"Any idea what that might be?" Tree asked.

"Piece of jewelry, maybe."

Judy's eyes narrowed as the implication of what the kid was suggesting became apparent. What's your name?" she asked.

"Dennis," came the reply.

"Dennis, supposing you have this 'piece of jewelry,' as you call it. What would you want for it?"

"A reward, I guess, you know, for it's safe return."

"Maybe you'd like to show us what you have before we make any offers," Judy said.

Dennis's grin widened as he shook his head. "No, you

don't. There's a dead man back there, a fact I guess you failed to mention."

"Didn't see any dead man," Dahlia interjected. "Have no idea what you're talking about."

"Yeah, well, he's back there. Deader than a doornail."

"You should call the police," Tree suggested.

"My friend Tree is one of those people who always wants to call the police," Dahlia said. She insinuated herself beside Dennis. "I don't think we need to do that, do you, Dennis?"

Dennis was obviously feeling the effect of Dahlia's closeness. "Guess it doesn't take a fool to know something about what people are willing to do for what I got on my hands. I know what I got and you know what I got, and if I get something in return then you get something. And that's the way the getting goes."

"I'm trying to think of what you could want," Dahlia purred.

"Money would do the trick."

"How much?"

"Ten thousand dollars might bring me around."

"All right," Judy said. "Let's go inside and I can wire you the money right away. As soon as that's done, you hand over what it is you have. How does that sound?"

"I can get the money right now?" The grin had evaporated, replaced by the hungry glow of expectation.

"Providing you have a bank account," Judy assured.

"You can do that?" Dennis appeared flabbergasted that he could come into that much money in such a short a time.

"I can," said Judy.

"But if you don't have what we're after, if you're jerking us around," Dahlia added ominously, "I swear you will end up back there with the body you found."

"No problem," said Dennis, unfolding his arms and beginning to move toward the garage. "I'm looking for money, not trouble."

"That's the spirit," Dahlia said.

As soon as Dennis provided his banking information, Judy transferred the ten thousand dollars. Dennis's eyes popped as he checked his account. "Jesus," he breathed.

"Your turn," Judy announced.

Dennis bent down to a small gray safe perched on a bottom shelf behind the counter. He pressed a series of numbers on the keypad and then opened the door and rummaged around inside for a moment before he brought out the tiara.

"Dunno what the big deal is," the kid said, rising to his feet and presenting the tiara to Judy. "Someone wear this at a beauty pageant or something?"

"Tell me how you came to be in possession of it." Tree confronted the kid.

Dennis gave another one of his shrugs, his eyes still bright with the excitement of his recent windfall. "Dude came around looking for a Mercedes that was a write-off. He seemed pretty anxious. I guess I only look dumb because it didn't take much to figure that something was up with that car. He came back all pissed and anxious because he couldn't find it. But after he left, I went back to have a look for myself. I found the car, no problem. When I looked in the glove compartment, I found that crown or whatever it is. I couldn't believe that's what the fella was looking for."

"But you held onto it."

"I figured the fella would come back and maybe we could make the sort of deal we just made."

"But he didn't come back," Tree said.

"That's the thing, he didn't. I wondered what was up when

I came in this morning. I went back and checked the car. That's when I found the guy's body."

"Dennis, here's what you're going to do," Tree said. "As soon as we're gone, you phone the police and tell them that you found a body."

"Okay," Dennis said. "I guess I should do that."

"What you *don't* tell them, you don't say anything about us or the tiara you found. Understand? If you do, the police will immediately take back your ten thousand dollars."

"And if they don't," Dahlia added. "I will come after you, and believe me, you don't want that."

"Don't worry," Dennis said. "In this job you don't tell the cops shit, about anything."

"That's what we like to hear," Dahlia said. She leaned forward and kissed him on the lips. The purr was back in her voice. "You're a good-looking man, Dennis. I like you." She kissed him again.

"You remind me of that actress," Dennis said huskily.

"What actress is that?" asked Dahlia."

"Trying to remember her name. Blond. She's dead now. Damn. I can't remember her name."

"Don't worry, Dennis," Dahlia said sweetly. She kissed him again.

Dennis's face glowed red.

26

Dahlia was in front as Judy drove south through a pine forest. That made it easy for her to slip the Glock out of her purse and hold it against the side of Judy's head. "Pull over," Dahlia ordered. She gave a quick glance to Tree in the back. "Tree, I want you to stay where you are. Don't try anything."

"What are you doing?" Judy, to her credit, despite the gun barrel pressed against her, kept her eyes on the road.

"What does it look like I'm doing?"

"It looks like you've decided to take the tiara for yourself."

"Just pull over, Judy."

"What? You're going to shoot me if I don't?"

"You know me."

"I'm driving at sixty-five miles an hour," Judy said tightly. "We're surrounded by trees. What do you think is going to happen if you shoot me?"

"Judy, don't argue. Pull over." There was a hard edge to Dahlia's voice.

"Dahlia, this is crazy," Tree said, not quite believing what he was witnessing.

"Shut up, Tree." Dahlia did not take her eyes off Judy. "I'm not telling you again, Judy, stop the car."

"You goddamn treacherous bitch," said Judy angrily.

"That's me, all right," Dahlia said. "Do it, Judy, stop the goddamn car."

Judy eased her foot off the gas. A couple of moments later, to Tree's relief, she pulled over onto the shoulder of the road.

"Out you go, the two of you," Dahlia ordered.

"You're leaving us in the middle of nowhere," Judy protested.

"You've got phones. Used them. Now get out."

When Judy reached for the door, Dahlia pulled the gun away enough so that Tree could lurch forward and grab her wrist. The gun went off with a loud bang, the bullet tearing a hole in the car's ceiling. With an animal-like shriek, Judy leapt onto a nonplussed Dahlia, knocking her back. The gun went flying. The two women issued loud grunts as they grappled together. Tree, ignored, scrambled out the back door.

Once outside, he fumbled open the driver's-side door and reached in and got his arm around Dahlia's neck. He did his best to ignore the prickly fire enveloping his ribs. Dahlia screamed loudly as he managed to pull the two women out of the car. They tumbled onto the road, Dahlia scratching at Judy's face. Judy smashed a fist into Dahlia's chin, a blow that knocked her back, allowing Judy to scamper around so that she was straddling her opponent.

Tree saw the open car door, the motor running, the two women issuing unintelligible animal-like sounds as they fought on the ground. He squeezed behind the wheel, slammed the door shut, shoved the car into drive and hit the gas. In a spray of gravel and dirt, Tree shot onto the road and sped away. Glancing in the rearview mirror he caught a quick view of the two women as they came apart, saw the flash of their stunned looks before he swept around a curve in the road. A feeling of exhilaration swept over him. He glanced at the tiara nestled on the floor of the passenger seat. Dahlia's gun lay nearby, partially hidden by Judy's handbag.

He slowed the car to a less attention-attracting seventy, forcing himself to calm down. Exhilaration was gone soon enough, however, replaced by the realization that he was no closer to Freddie than before and maybe even further away. A familiar question rose up and began to nag at him: Now what?

He did not have a lot of time before Judy and the lethal Dahlia reconciled their mutual antagonism and came after him or, more accurately, the tiara.

A service station came into view in a clearing among the pine trees not far from the cutoff to I-75. He turned into the graveled lot and then leaned down to retrieve the gun and the handbag. Rummaging through the bag, he found the car's key fob. Judy's billfold contained a thousand dollars in cash. He discovered in a side pocket an old-fashioned address book in which Judy actually took time to write down names, addresses, and phone numbers.

It was a long shot. O for Orcus. A telephone number and an address. A single O in black ink beside a Naples address.

Then, a wild thought…

Under V, there were the initials VP in similar black ink. Beside the initials, a sprawling telephone number: 7 495 606 38 05. No, Tree thought, it couldn't be…*that* simple…

Judy's phone was in her purse. The code to open it turned out to be scrawled across the opening page of the address book. He poked out the number listed beside VP. A flurry of clicking sounds was followed by a distant electronic ringing. Then someone picked up the phone and said in Russian, "Da?"

"Hello," Tree said. "Am I speaking to President Putin?"

There was a pause on the other end. "Who is this?" in English.

"I'm a friend of Orcus. Is this President Putin?"

Another pause, this one even longer. "The President is not here at the moment. Who is this speaking, please."

"Like I said, a friend of Orcus."

"I know of no such person," said the voice on the other end of the line.

"My name is Tree Callister. I would like you to deliver a message to President Putin."

"And what is this message?"

"Please inform him that I have the Alexandra Tiara, the object that I believe he is looking for. He must contact his friend Orcus and tell him that I will turn over this object in exchange for the woman Orcus is holding."

In some confusion, the voice asked: "Who is this again?"

"Tree Callister. I can be reached at this number."

He closed the phone and then worked himself cautiously out of the car, wondering about what he had just done. Whoever answered the phone wasn't Vladimir Putin, but at least his call was answered. Would his message reach the Russian president? Who knew how many crank calls were received each day at the Kremlin. But then would any Russian in the current repressive climate dare to make such a call?

He limped into the gas station, his body sharply reminding him that it was still hurting everywhere. The attendant behind a plexiglass shield looked like he had grown into his seat. Tree presented a cellophane-wrapped ham sandwich and a bottle of water.

"How you doin' there pardner?" the attendant asked, not unsympathetically when he got a look at how banged up Tree appeared to be. "Everything okay?"

"I just called the president of Russia," Tree said.

The attendant nodded sagely. "Well, how's he doing?"

"I couldn't get hold of him."

"Yeah, well, people in power. Hard to get through to them," said the attendant. He gave Tree back the change from a twenty-dollar bill. "You take care of yourself—and if you get hold of the president, say howdy from me."

"Got it," said Tree.

As he hobbled outside, Judy's phone began playing a swelling orchestral version of "Some Enchanted Evening." He leaned against the side of the car as he raised the phone to his ear. "Mr. Callister?" inquired a voice with a mid-Atlantic accent. Not the same voice as before, thought Tree. He said, "Yes, I'm Callister."

"Mr. Callister, I am calling you on behalf of my superiors…"

"Who are you?"

"I am the person you need to talk to."

"Would one of those superiors be President Putin?" Tree interjected.

"I've been instructed to have a word with you, Mr. Callister." Tree's question was ignored.

"A word that includes the whereabouts of my wife?"

"I need first of all to confirm that you are in possession of the Alexandra Tiara, the beloved crown that was stolen from the Russian people many years ago, and which we are anxious to recover."

"I have the tiara," Tree said. "What about my wife?"

"If you have what you say you have, an arrangement can be made."

"What kind of arrangement?"

"We will be in touch."

An electronic click signalled that the call had ended.

27

Tree waited around for the next hour expecting a call back with further instructions. There was nothing.

"You get hold of them Russians of yours?" asked the attendant when Tree went back in for more water.

"Not yet," Tree said.

"You tell them Russians if they decide to invade Florida, we're ready for 'em," the attendant said firmly. "Tell 'em everyone in this state is armed, locked and loaded and ready for anything."

"I'll be sure to let them know," Tree said. He paid the attendant for more gas and then went outside and filled the tank.

Still, no one called.

Tree got back into the car to escape the afternoon heat. He turned on the air-conditioning full force. He allowed the cold air to waft over him as he drank more water. With every part of his body inflamed, he felt as though he was running out of options. His eyes fell on Judy's address book lying on the passenger seat. He picked up the book and found the page he was looking for.

The house at 2234 Gordon Drive in Naples was on a corner lot behind a high wall. He parked at the curb, not far from a wrought iron entrance gate blocking a sweeping stone drive that he soon discovered was locked. The street appeared deserted. Only the sound of cicadas broke a silence that was almost ominous. Everyone had gone to the moon, Tree thought.

Or so it seemed.

In the old days, his more limber days, Tree might have tried to climb over the wall. Not that he was ever particularly athletic, but back then he might have succeeded. Considering he could barely make it along the street, those days were gone.

Long gone…

If they were—and they most definitely were—then how could he access the house? Ring the bell that was part of the intercom system attached to the wall adjacent to the entrance gate? A good idea that he tried. There was no response.

He slowly made his way around the block to an iron gate built into an archway in the wall. Tree tried the handle. The gate creaked inward.

Beyond the wall a fantasy world, Naples chapter, began with an expanse of emerald green lawn sweeping to the ocean, interrupted every so often by gloriously colored flowerbeds. Through the afternoon haze, tennis courts were visible. The main house was a mini-Versailles with terra-cotta roof tiles that probably never occurred to Lous XIV. He stood by the lake-sized pool. The silence was overwhelming.

Tree crossed the pool deck to open French doors. Inside, a pool table dominated a game room. Tree entered a state-of-the-art kitchen that was as large as most people's houses.

The music of "Some Enchanted Evening" erupted suddenly from Judy's phone. He withdrew it from his pocket. "Mr. Callister," said the now-familiar voice. "My apologies for not getting back to you sooner. Where are you now?"

"I'm in an empty house on Gordon Drive in Naples."

"What are you doing there, Mr. Callister?"

"I'm trying to find my wife."

"You were supposed to stay put until I got back to you."

"What about my wife?"

"She is not there. Please leave the house."

"But—"

"Get out, Mr. Callister—now!"

The call broke off again.

28

Tree slipped back onto the street. At first, he didn't notice the small man in a pale linen sports jacket wearing a white Panama hat. He leaned against the side of a convertible Volkswagen Beetle. He was holding the Alexandra Tiara.

"Hey, there," the small man said as Tree approached. "That's some house, isn't it? Too big for me, though. Guys like Prince, Michael Jackson, and Mathew Perry, they sit in houses like that, alone and miserable, with nothing to do except ingest various drugs. They end up dead in those houses. Not for me. I visit from time to time, but I mostly stay out of there. I may sell it before too long."

He showed Tree the tiara he was holding. "I took the liberty of retrieving it from your car." He favored Tree with a sunny smile that exploded across a florid red face. If you didn't know better, you might be tempted to tell him what you wanted for Christmas. "You look like you're suffering a bit, partner, if you don't mind my saying."

"A few aches and pains," Tree allowed. He kept his eyes on the tiara in the small man's hands. "Mind telling me what do you think you're doing with that?"

"Age. Gets to all of us." The small man's face brightened, as though he had a sudden, delightful thought. "Say, you look like you could use a ride, make it a little easier on yourself. Why don't you hop in? I've got the old Beetle right here."

"I have my own car," Tree said. "I'll take that tiara back and be on my way."

"You'd better ride with me, Mr. Callister." The small man

nonchalantly tossed the tiara into the backseat of the Beetle. "That way you can keep an eye on that piece of jewelry."

Tree gave him a long look. "Who are you?"

"Someone you should take a ride with."

"My mother taught me that I should never accept a ride from strangers."

"However, you want to see your wife, so I think you should come with me," the small man said sensibly. He turned and opened the Beetle's passenger's-side door.

"I don't know who you are," Tree said.

"My friends here in Naples know me as amiable Damian Fargo."

"And your enemies?"

"They know me as Orcus."

"You're Orcus?" Tree couldn't keep the disbelief out of his voice.

"You were expecting someone in black wearing a cape?"

"Not the cape, necessarily," Tree said.

"Why don't you hop in, Mr. Callister?"

Tree thought about it and then leaned down to get in the Beetle, trying not to grunt with pain. As they drove away, he heard the sound of police sirens growing louder. Presumably they were headed for the Gordon Drive mansion.

"I'm not what anyone expects," Orcus offered with a grin as he navigated the Beetle through Naples streets. "But that's a good thing."

"Is it?"

"You're not exactly anyone's idea of a private detective, either," Orcus said, giving Tree a quick sideways glance.

"I'm retired."

"Are you? From what I understand, you're not acting very retired."

"I'm trying to get to my wife," Tree said. He indicated the tiara in the backseat. "You've got what you want. Now I want her back."

"We're going to have some lunch and then we can talk," Orcus said.

"I'm tired of talking," Tree said tightly.

Orcus swung the car onto a street lined with modest white-washed bungalows. He stopped at the end. "Here we are," he said.

He got out of the car, making sure to pluck the tiara out of the back before leading Tree along a stone walkway to a frost-ed-glass front door. He opened the door and Tree followed him into a sparsely furnished living room. One wall was dominated by a framed photograph of palm trees overlooking a tranquil sea beneath a blue sky full of fluffy clouds. A stooped woman hobbled into view. Her shoulder-length hair was dyed black. The deep lines etched in her face gave her the appearance of permanent agitation. Her eyes were dark and fierce. A devil's eyes, thought Tree.

"You're late, Damian." She spoke angrily in a thick eastern accent. "Lunch is getting cold."

"Apologies, Mama Alina." He turned to Tree. "I'd like to introduce you to Mr. Tremain Callister. I have told you about him. Tree, this is my stepmother, my beloved Mama Alina"

Mama Alina looked anything but beloved as she set the devil's rapacious eyes on the tiara. "Is that it?"

"What do you think?"

"Lunchtime," pronounced Mama Alina.

The two men followed her into a kitchen to where a table had been set. They seated themselves while Mama Alina went to the stove and opened the oven door. Warm baking smells filled the air.

"I hope you like spinach quiche," Orcus said. Tree noticed that he kept the Panama hat on. "It's one of Mama Alina's specialties."

Mama Alina silently went to work cutting the quiche into slices and placing two of them on white plates. She unceremoniously plopped one of the plates in front of Tree. He stared at it, trying to decide if it was poisoned.

"It's not poisoned," Orcus said pleasantly, as if reading his mind.

Tree gingerly picked up a fork, cut off a piece, and stuck it in his mouth. The other two watched him closely. He nodded. "Very good."

That seemed to satisfy Orcus. He bit into his quiche. Mama Alina did not seem so convinced. She continued to eye Tree as he nervously ate more.

"Tell me if you want another slice," she said finally.

"This is good, thanks," Tree said.

"Delicious," added Orcus sticking another forkful into his mouth. He pointed his fork at Mama Alina who, Tree couldn't help notice, had not served herself. "Tell him about the love of your life."

Mama Alina waved her hand dismissively. "He does not want to hear this."

"Yes, I'm sure he does," Orcus pushed. "Tell him."

Mama Alina sat back with a resigned sigh. "Many years ago, I was a teenager arriving in Moscow from Sergiyev Posad, a beautiful village north of Moscow. Here is the monastery of St. Sergius. It is the most sacred place in the Russian Orthodox Church. This is why I had to leave," she said. "I was young. I was not interested in anything sacred."

"In Moscow, I was very lonely at first but then my sister introduced me to a young man, blond, very handsome. We were immediately drawn to one another. But he was very mysterious, enigmatic. He said he worked for the government, but no more than that. I was falling in love, so what he did was of no real importance, other than it was government, so I knew he had a secure position. He liked to drink vodka. We both liked to drink vodka. Ordinarily, he was very disciplined. He drank but never too much, never out of control like so many other young Russian men. But then one night, very late, he was not so much in control, he let his guard down, so to speak. He revealed to me who he really was…"

"Who was he, Mama Alina?" Orcus's voice was full of excitement. "Tell Tree who he was."

"My Vladimir," she said wistfully. "My wonderful Vladimir was a KGB agent. A very powerful man as it turned out. The man I loved. My Vladimir."

There was actually a tear in Mama Alina's eyes as she revealed this.

"Vladimir Putin," breathed Tree.

"How could there be any other Vladimir?" put in Orcus.

"The love of my life," repeated Mama Alina. "When Vladimir says to me, 'Alina, you must go to America. You must work for us. You must stay very quiet as you do this, but always you will work for us.'"

"Mama Alina became an American citizen," Orcus cut in. "She even achieved that most American of goals, she married a millionaire—"

"A multimillionaire," corrected Alina. "Maybe even a billionaire. Who knows? He was a terrible man. A drunk."

"A Fargo," interjected Orcus.

"A good-for-nothing family in my estimation. You have

only to look at my stepson, the so-called general."

"My stepbrother," interrupted Orcus. "Not as bad as Mama makes him out to be, but I do have to keep an eye on him. A bit of craziness runs in that family, unfortunately—and lies. Ares likes to make himself out to be this military man, a general. He was never a general.

"Nonetheless," Orcus continued, "thanks to Alina's belief in me and her endless generosity, I have been able to create the organization dedicated to saving this country, fighting to remake it into the greatest empire the world has ever known."

"And it isn't that, already?" Tree asked.

"It could be better," Orcus replied.

"With Russian help?"

"Why not?" said Orcus.

"I can think of a lot of reasons, but none of them has anything to do with a tiara."

"I will return it to my Vladimir," stated Mama Alina with certainty. "Once he sees what I have done, we will be together again."

Tree gave her a long look. "You mean to say all of this is about your desire to rekindle a teenage romance with Vladimir Putin?"

"That is enough?" Mama Alina erupted. "That is everything!"

Orcus didn't say anything. Mama Alina's eyes were alive as she reached over and picked up the tiara. She held it up, her deeply lined face began to darken and the anticipatory light went out of her eyes. "This is it! Finally!" The words were spat out of her twisted mouth. "It is mine. The Alexandra Tiara!"

29

With surprising agility, Mama Alina leapt up to the kitchen counter, and yanked open a drawer. She swirled around, a long-bladed kitchen knife raised in her hand, springing at Tree.

He ducked away but not fast enough to stop the knife blade slicing through his shoulder. He had the presence of mind to land a fist against Mama Alina's enraged face. She screamed and staggered back, dropping the knife. Orcus was on his feet, having somehow found the gun he aimed at Tree. He pulled the trigger. Nothing happened. "Shit," said Orcus. Tree dropped to the floor, picking up the knife. Orcus came around the table. Tree managed to get hold of the old woman and haul her to her feet. She was babbling incoherently as he held her struggling skin-and-bones body, pressing the knife against her throat.

Across the way Orcus stopped. "Drop the gun," ordered Tree. "Do it or I swear I will slit her throat."

"I don't think it's working anyway," Orcus said sadly.

"Then drop it."

"Kill him!" shrieked Mama Alina by way of offering Orcus an alternative suggestion. "Kill him!"

"At the moment, Mama, I'm afraid that's not possible," Orcus said regretfully. He lowered the gun to the kitchen table, keeping his eyes firmly on Tree. "There you go, Tree," he said, straightening. "I'm cooperating with you." He looked at Mama Alina. "Listen, my mother may have overreacted. The tiara, as you can imagine, is most important to her…"

"Do not talk to him," raged Mama Alina. "Kill him!"

"Please, Mama, you must be calm."

"I am not calm," she screamed. "I say kill!"

Orcus addressed Tree. "I believe it is not too late to reach agreement. A way so that bygones can be bygones."

"The way that returns my wife to me," Tree said.

"Don't listen to him!" Mama Alina shouted hysterically, struggling against the knife at her throat. Seeing that Tree was distracted, Orcus lunged for the gun on the table. Tree knocked Alina aside and got to the gun ahead of Orcus. Gun in hand, he spun around as Alina came at him. He whipped the barrel across the side of Alina's head. The high-pitched screaming was cut off immediately. She dropped to the floor.

Orcus smashed into Tree, knocking him back against the kitchen counter. Tree tried to get the gun into a position where he could use it to knock Orcus away—couldn't quite manage it. Taking a page from Dahlia's instruction book when it came to a fast resolution of a tight situation, he pulled the trigger. This time the gun went off. The bullet struck Orcus in his right foot.

Roaring with pain, he dropped to the floor beside the unconscious Mama Alina. His Panama hat rolled away.

Tree pushed himself away from the counter, blood seeping from his shoulder wound, aware of how weak he was feeling.

Holding onto the gun, he made his way through the living room. He managed to get the front door open, weaker than ever. He stumbled out into bright sunshine, blinking as Judy Markov came toward him.

"Don't shoot," she said.

30

O n the one hand," said the Orange Man, "you shot the son-of-a-bitch. You acted like a man for a change instead of a wimp moping around the countryside whining about your wife. On the other hand, you shot the son of a bitch in the foot. Pussies shoot people in the foot. Personally, I would have gut shot him. That's what a man would do. But hey, Tree, you're not much of a man, are you?"

The Orange Man wore a red Speedo bathing suit. His large belly glistened with sweat and suntan lotion, rising and falling with a mesmerizing rhythm as he lay on a chaise lounge beside a vast swimming pool.

"I shot someone after pistol-whipping an old lady, I feel sick about it," admitted Tree. He sat on a chair not far from where the Orange Man was splayed out in all his glory.

"Lot of good it did you," the Orange Man said disdainfully. "You still can't find your wife. You're useless."

"But I'm doing all I can to find her," Tree said desperately.

"But you keep failing, darling," Freddie said as she sauntered across the pool deck. She looked amazing in the red bikini that matched the Orange Man's Speedo.

"I love you, Freddie," Tree pleaded. "You know how much I love you."

"That doesn't make a whole lot of difference if you can't find me," Freddie said. She slipped onto the chaise lounge beside the Orange Man. She ran her hand over his vast stomach as she snuggled against him, keeping her eyes on Tree. "You've had your chance, Tree. I've decided to move on, to be with a real man who knows how to treat a woman like me."

"Why don't you get lost, Tree? Your wife and I have business to attend to."

"No," cried Tree, "you can't do this. You can't take my wife away. You can't—"

"Tree!" called a voice. "For God's sake, get hold of yourself—"

Tree, breathing hard, forced his eyes open. Judy stood over him with an impatient expression. The Alexandra Tiara was perched on her head. "Judy—" was all he could rally himself enough to say.

"What do you think, Tree?" She lifted her hands to frame the tiara. "Looks pretty good on me."

"You found it?"

"I *retrieved* it." She removed the tiara and placed it on a nearby counter. "That was quite the mess you left behind."

Tree managed to raise himself onto his elbows enough to look groggily around. "Where am I?"

"A mobile home in a trailer park that somehow managed to survive Ian," Judy stated. "Not my first choice for accommodation, but the safest."

"But how—?" Tree started in a confused voice.

"Not to worry, Tree, I don't mind saving your ass once again. Also, I forgive you for driving off and leaving me stranded with that double-dealing bitch Red Dahlia."

"Forgiveness comes with the tiara, I suppose." Tree lay back on the bed in what looked to be a good-sized mobile home. "Given the circumstances, the two of you fighting…"

"When I finally disentangled myself from her, I assumed you would have gone through my purse and found my address book. When I got to Gordon Drive, there was my car outside the house and inside a lot of dead bodies. I decided to try my luck with Mama Alina, the brains and the financing behind Orcus's organization. Sure enough, they were in the process of doing what I was pretty sure they would do—killing you. I'm amazed they didn't succeed." She gave him a speculative look. "Did you really shoot, Orcus?"

"In the foot," Tree said.

"That would do the trick," Judy said. "It kept you alive, at least until I turned up to once more save the day—and, like I said, your sorry ass."

"I suppose I should thank you," Tree said morosely.

"That would be nice," Judy allowed.

"Not that it gets me any closer to finding Freddie."

"I thought Orcus would have had her," Judy said.

Tree shook his head.

"I found your pal Vlady's phone number in your address book," Tree explained. "When I called, someone answered the phone."

"But not Vlady?"

"No."

"It was probably Boris. Boris Volkova."

"Is he behind all this?"

"It makes sense," Judy said. "Like I told you before, Volkova was my liaison with Vlady in Moscow. A very dangerous and conniving individual. He is also the brains behind Orcus and Mama Alina. Those dead bodies on Gordon Drive, undoubtedly Volkova's doing. He must have been after Orcus—and the tiara."

"Orcus didn't seem all that upset," Tree offered.

"Possibly because you come along with what he and Mama Alina and everyone else under the sun is after."

"As soon as Mama Alina had it, that's when everything blew up and she tried to kill me."

"Honestly, Alina is so predictable. When she gets what she wants from you, she kills you." Judy added sardonically, "Who would have suspected she would meet her match with you, Tree."

"Not me, that's for sure," Tree said.

He eased himself out of bed, setting loose fiery knife blades of pain that took great pleasure in ravaging his body with a particular emphasis on the shoulder where Mama Alina had sliced him. From what Tree could see of his shoulder, Judy had done a fair job of dressing the wound. That didn't lessen the pain.

"Thank you for doing this," Tree said, indicating his wounded shoulder.

"Old ladies, thank goodness, don't have the strength to get the knife blades in too deep. I managed to get the bleeding stopped, cleaned and closed the wound, and got you bandaged up, drawing on my first aid training from my days in Girl Guides."

"I don't think I knew you were ever in Girl Guides," said Tree.

"As I have said many times, there is so much about me you never knew—so much you never cared to know."

"I should say something like that's not true."

"No, you shouldn't, Tree."

"No," Tree replied quietly, "I shouldn't."

Under the reviving hot spray of the cramped shower in the mobile home, careful not to get his bandaged shoulder wet, Tree began to feel better. Stepping from the shower, he went so far as to begin to believe he might be able to face the day, to pull himself together to continue the search for Freddie. But then as he dressed in the clothes he had been wearing for days now, a combination of depression and fatigue washed over him.

He felt as though he had come to an impasse, with no idea as to Freddie's whereabouts, increasingly worried that he was too late, too old, too stupid, too anything, to save her.

He came back into the mobile home's sitting area. Judy was nowhere in sight. She had left her phone on the table. He picked up the phone. He had already called the number. All he had to do was redial it and wait for someone to answer. Maybe nothing. Maybe something.

The phone began to ring. It continued to ring and ring. No one answered. Eventually, he gave up. Deeply disappointed, he slumped onto the couch, everything in his body beginning to hurt again. Particularly his broken heart.

Then, suddenly, Judy's phone came alive, vibrating on the table followed by the orchestral swell of "Some Enchanted Evening." Tree grabbed for the phone. "Hello?"

"Tree?" a breathless Freddie said.

"Freddie! God, Freddie," Tree said anxiously.

"I'm okay, Tree, I'm fine," Freddie said.

"Where are you?"

For a moment there was silence on the other end of the line.

"Freddie, tell me where you are."

"I'm in Moscow," Freddie said.

31

Tree was certain he hadn't heard her correctly. "What did you say?"

Instead of Freddie's answer, Tree heard what sounded like someone taking the phone away from her. Then: "Mr. Callister." The smooth, authoritative voice came through with clarity.

"Volkova." The name was out of Tree's mouth in a rush of breath.

There was a long silence before the voice said, "You have mistaken me for someone else."

"No, I haven't," Tree said firmly. "Put my wife back on the phone."

"Your wife is quite safe, Mr. Callister. But naturally, she would prefer to be reunited with you. The question is, what are you willing to do in order to make this happen."

"Anything," Tree blurted. "I'll do anything."

"We only require the return of the Alexandra Tiara. I am assuming you can deliver it."

"Yes, I have it," Tree assured anxiously.

"I propose an exchange. You give us the tiara and we will arrange for you to be reunited with your wife."

"How? How do we do this?"

"We suggest a meeting in neutral territory, safer for both sides."

"Where?"

"We are prepared to do this in Vienna."

"Vienna?"

"It's in Austria," said the voice dryly.

"I know where it is."

"Then we will meet there in three days."

"But—"

"Check into the Hotel Sacher. We will be in touch."

The voice was gone.

Freddie was alive!

He had heard her voice. There was no doubting it was her. He *could* get her back, it was possible. All he had to do was get to Vienna, a city where he'd had trouble before, in three days. No problem.

Except...

There *was* a problem. How was he to get to Vienna within the allotted time? Would Judy ever agree to this arrangement? Or would she suspect—as he should—that this was some kind of trick, and Freddie wouldn't be in Vienna at all.

The opening door signaling Judy's return drew him out of his reverie. She was not alone. A tall, lanky, rather professorial type crouched in behind her. His brown hair was pushed back to show off a tanned angular face; the face of an academic, Tree thought, of someone whose authority had never been questioned. Certainly unlike Tree's face. The visitor's slim frame might have been more at home in a well-tailored suit, but he was slumming among the curious natives of Southwest Florida, and so he wore an untucked white cotton shirt, faded jeans and Sketchers.

"Good," said Judy, "you're off the phone."

How did she know he was on the phone? Tree wondered.

The tall thin man's head was inches away from scraping the mobile home's ceiling as he held out a big hand to Tree. "Apologies for barging in like this, Tree—do you mind if I call you Tree?"

Tree ignored the outstretched hand, and shot Judy a look.

"Tree, I want you to meet Travis Dunn."

"I've heard a lot about you, Tree," said Dunn. Which could mean almost anything, Tree thought. None of it good.

"I still don't know who you are," Tree said.

"Travis is with the Central Intelligence Agency," Judy said. She added unnecessarily, "The CIA."

Tree looked at her in dismay. "Are you working with the CIA?"

"Not by choice," Judy said grimly.

Travis Dunn had taken a seat across from Tree. "Judy has decided that she doesn't want to spend the rest of her life in prison for spying on the United States for the Russians," he said agreeably, as if he dealt with people all the time who were caught spying for the Russians.

"Which I wasn't doing," Judy put in firmly.

Dunn raised a cynical eyebrow before saying, "Let's put that aside for the time being."

"I'm just saying," persisted Judy.

Dunn turned his attention to Tree. "I'm sorry about your wife," he said it as though he might actually be sorry. "I've come here to work with you to bring about her safe return."

"I just spoke to her. She's being held in Moscow."

This didn't seem to come as a surprise to Dunn. Tree was getting the impression nothing came as a surprise to Dunn. "We've been liaising with Judy for some time," he said. "We are up to speed with events involving the Alexandra Tiara. We have suspected for some time that Ms. Stayner is being held by Russian authorities."

Tree gave Judy an accusatory look. "You might have told me."

"I haven't had a whole lot of choice about what I can say

or cannot say," Judy said. "If we help these bastards and do as they tell me, I stay out of jail. If I don't…well, we're both in trouble."

"We?"

"The Russians are demanding that you return the tiara," Dunn said. "We are going to help you do that."

"I don't want to do anything that will jeopardize my getting my wife back," Tree said.

"Yes, but I doubt you can accomplish that alone," Dunn said. "However, we can help you make sure that happens."

"Why would you do that?"

"Maybe because we're the good guys," Dunn said without irony.

"Are you?"

"Yeah, on occasion we are. This could be one of those times."

"Not as far as I'm concerned," Judy said, barely keeping the snarl out of her voice.

"In return for what?" Tree addressed the CIA agent.

"That was Boris Volkova you were talking to on the phone. I believe he's already tried to kill you. We believe he was also behind the murder of Gladys Demchuk. We've been trying to get to him for years. Now I think we can do it, and at the same time put the final piece of a puzzle together that has been years in the making—the destruction of a Russian sleeper cell here in America that has been fronting as an ultra-right-wing organization."

"Legio Three and Orcus," said Tree.

"I understand that you have just put the despicable Orcus and his equally despicable stepmother in the hospital. Good work, incidentally. The two of them are the founders and funders of Legio Three. There are others as well, but right now, everything and everyone stays in place, business as usual so as not to alert the Russians until we are finished in Vienna."

Dunn looked at his watch. "That's about it. Judy has all the details but the plan is to get the two of you to Vienna late tomorrow and—"

"Wait a minute," Judy interrupted irately. "You didn't say anything about me going."

"Didn't I? I was sure I did," Dunn said vaguely. "It will look less suspicious if you are there. After all, you're supposed to be benefiting from the return of the tiara, putting you back in Putin's good books and all that."

"Except if this doesn't work, they will be only too happy to put an end to me," Judy said morosely. "It's a lot easier to do that in Vienna than it is here."

"Then let's make sure it works," said Dunn peremptorily. "We will get this done, Mr. Callister. We will get your wife back. Not to worry."

The signal, Tree thought, to start worrying.

As soon as Travis Dunn left, Judy broke down in tears. In the years they were together, Tree had never seen her cry. She sat sobbing, her body bent forward so she could bury her face in her hands as though she didn't want Tree to see her crying.

He wasn't sure how to react. "Are you all right?" he ventured.

"No, for Christ's sake, I'm not." She glared at him fiercely. "Does it look like I'm all right? Christ! My life is ruined. I've been blackmailed into being a government informant or, worse, a double agent when I was never an agent at all!"

"In fairness, Judy, you have been pretty close with your pal Vlady. Not a good look these days."

"Now, I've got to take you to Vienna," she continued tearfully. "If I'm not already dead as a result of this, they're sure to get me in Vienna when they find out what I've been up to."

"I get the impression that Agent Dunn didn't just walk in off the street. You've been dealing with him for a while, haven't you?"

"The FBI jumped me shortly after the hurricane and the fire that destroyed my house. They said they had all sorts of shit on me and that I was probably going to jail, unless—"

"Unless you cooperated with them."

"They knew about Vlady's obsession with the Alexandra Tiara, and they knew I had it."

"Unless you told them it had been lost in the fire."

"Which I actually thought might be true…"

"But you had to find out for sure," Tree suggested, "and since you were afraid the FBI and the CIA were watching you, you couldn't very well go to the house yourself, so you convinced me, your patsy of an ex-husband, to get it."

"Well, I wouldn't exactly call you a patsy—easily manipulated would be more like it. And," she added, "helpful, I have to admit."

"Except it got a whole lot more complicated than just me picking up the tiara. It turned out all sorts of people wanted it, including Red Dahlia and Sergei Markov."

"Sergei knew that his brother Alexei had the tiara and that after Alexei's death I inherited it. Nothing has happened the way it was supposed to. Certainly not the disappearance of your wife."

She reached for a box of tissues on the counter. "But then I guess it works out for those CIA bastards."

Tree eyed her narrowly. "How does it work out for the CIA?"

Judy grew tense. "Never mind," she said airily.

"Judy, what aren't you telling me?"

"I'm telling you everything you need to know."

"I don't think you are."

"Look, do you want to get your wife back or not?"

"Of course—"

"Then quit asking so many goddamn questions!" Judy snapped. She used the tissue to wipe furiously at her falling tears before she stormed out.

32

En route into the city from Vienna International Airport, Tree said, "'I never knew Vienna between the wars, and I am too young to remember the old Vienna with its Strauss music and its bogus easy charm.'"

"What's that?" Judy asked irritably.

"Graham Greene," Tree said. "*The Third Man*. It always brings back memories of the last time I was in Vienna."

"I have no idea what you're talking about." Judy was lost in her own thoughts, staring out the window at the gray industrial Vienna that lay beyond the city center.

"Post-war Vienna is the setting for Greene's book as well as the classic movie with Orson Welles," Tree explained. "When I was here years ago, it was also the setting for a nasty encounter with my half-brother."

"Whatever," said Judy disinterestedly. She had been morose and uncommunicative ever since the meeting with CIA agent Travis Dunn. The confident, controlled American oligarch had disappeared into the fog of her new reality: Judy had lost everything and was now under the thumb of American law enforcement. Cooperating with them was all that was keeping her out of prison.

"Goddamn Vienna—*Wien*," she murmured, using the German pronunciation of the city. As though on cue in support of her depression, it started to rain.

"If it's any consolation, I don't feel much differently," Tree said.

"Russian agents who don't shave regularly sitting around

eating schnitzel, plotting ways to assassinate people like me. Americans in Brooks Brothers suits who shave twice a day paying off young women to steal secrets from the Russians you could probably find on the Internet. It's the bad old days all over again—and just as meaningless."

"And yet here we are," noted Tree.

"What's more, the food is lousy."

"Unless you like schnitzel," Tree said.

"I hate schnitzel," replied Judy glumly.

Their cab entered the heart of modern-day Vienna, a series of massive blocks obscured by the drizzling rain. The Hotel Sacher was a blur save an ornate entranceway overhung with flags and lit in golden hues so the rich would have no trouble finding it. To Tree, the grandly luxurious hotel remained much the same as it had when he and Freddie had checked in years before. Judy may have been down on her luck, but she still managed to give orders to the doormen and the porters hustling behind with her luggage, a general imperiously crossing already-conquered terrain.

When Judy finished, she marched back to Tree. "I'm going to my room, taking a shower, and ordering room service."

"Okay, we're here," Tree said. "But now what?"

"Now we wait," Judy said. "And we try not to eat the Sacher torte." She started away, a knot of porters scrambling behind. Then she paused. The porters came to an abrupt stop. She returned to Tree. "One more thing. Keep an eye out."

"For what?"

"Anything. I don't trust Travis Dunn and I certainly don't trust Boris Volkova. You're in Vienna. Don't trust anyone."

"What about you, Judy? Can I trust you?"

"Why, Tree," she replied adopting a look as close to coquettishness as Judy was ever likely to get. "You know me."

Unfortunately, he did, Tree thought to himself as he watched Judy sashay off followed by her luggage-bearing porters. If Judy didn't want to attract attention in Vienna, she wasn't doing a very good job of it.

He stared around the lobby. The tourist types gathered in a corner looked innocent enough. The occupants of the plush chairs, chatting and sipping cocktails, looked too old and too comfortable to be international spies. But then who knew? Graham Greene would know, Tree reflected as he headed for the elevator. This was his territory after all. But he was nowhere to be seen.

The heavy drapes in his fifth-floor suite were open, affording him a view of the Vienna State Opera across the street. To fully enjoy the window view, however, Tree would have had to navigate around the king-size bed where Red Dahlia lay. She did not have any clothes on. Judy had warned him to keep his eyes open, but even she couldn't have imagined this. Or maybe she could, which was why she warned him.

"Appropriate, don't you think?" Dahlia said.

"How is that?" Tree asked, dropping the single piece of luggage he had brought with him, trying to maintain the cool necessary when unexpectedly encountering a naked woman in one's hotel room.

"Right out of my favorite spy movie, *From Russia with Love*. James Bond comes into his hotel room and finds Tania Romanova in his bed. All she's wearing is a black ribbon."

"But you're not wearing a ribbon," Tree said, keeping his distance, as though the area around the bed might be radioactive. "And I'm not James Bond."

"No ribbon, no Bond," Dahlia said disappointedly, rolling

over on her side to face Tree. "We will have to make the best of it."

"Do you mind telling me how you got in here?"

"The passionate wife who's just arrived in town and wants to surprise her husband." She paused. "I am known for my ability to talk anyone into anything—particularly when it comes to men." The purr was back in her voice.

"What are you trying to talk me into, Dahlia?"

"Not trying to talk you into anything," she said, sitting up on the bed and swinging her legs onto the floor. "I'm here to talk you *out* of something."

"Like what?"

Dahlia got up from the bed and went over to the chair where she had draped her clothes. "What you're going to do, Tree, you're going to wait until I get dressed, and then you're going to come with me." Dahlia was slipping into her panties as she spoke.

"I'm not going anywhere with you," Tree said, watching Dahlia zip up a short black skirt and then reach for a blouse. "I'm dead tired. I want sleep and you out of here."

"Sorry Tree, that's not going to happen."

An adjoining door opened and two big men stepped in. They hadn't shaved for a while and you could believe from the size of them that they had spent a lot of time eating schnitzel.

"I want you to meet my friends," Dahlia said. "They can get very rough if they have to." She seated herself on the bed to slip into a pair of expensive-looking high heels.

The men fixed squinty eyes on Tree. They did not say anything that would contradict Dahlia's assertion. The looks of them said everything.

Fully dressed, Dahlia rose to her feet, smoothing her skirt, addressing the two friends. "Do either of you happen to have a cigarette?"

"You have stopped smoking, I understand," said the taller friend in thickly accented English.

"I don't know who told you that."

"Her daughter doesn't want her smoking," interjected Tree.

The smaller friend jerked a thumb in Tree's direction. "You see? Your friend has your best interests at heart."

"I very much doubt that," Dahlia said. "Let's get out of here. We'll take the stairs."

"Where are we going?" demanded Tree.

"To see the sights of Vienna after dark," Dahlia said. She swayed past them and headed for the door. She opened it, paused as though struck by a thought and then turned to Tree. "I just want you to know…"

"What's that, Dahlia?"

"I had no intention of screwing you."

"Never crossed my mind," Tree said.

Lying.

33

A black Bentley—could there be any other color in the spy-versus-spy city that apparently was Vienna?—had been parked in the rain at the side entrance adjacent to the Café Mozart. As soon as he was in the back, one of Dahlia's friends handed him a black hood—another necessary cliché, Tree thought.

"Put it on," Dahlia ordered from the front.

"I've never been to Vienna so it's not as though I have any idea where we are going," Tree lied, holding the hood.

"Do as I say," Dahlia said.

Tree yanked the hood over his head. The world dropped into darkness. There was the sound of the car's motor starting up. A moment later, they were off. Tree had experienced this before, the sensation of moving without seeing, in the company of people who in all probability did not have his best interests at heart. There was a tightening of his stomach muscles, along with feelings of increasing anxiousness.

Dahlia remained uncustomarily quiet during the drive through the streets of Vienna. Her silence, the low hum of the car's engine, the swoosh of the outside wind, the tires against wet pavement, only added to the tension. They drove for about twenty minutes, by Tree's estimation, before the Bentley came to a stop.

He heard the sound of doors opening and then the passenger door beside him. He was gently guided outside, feeling rain thump against the hood. Someone pulled the hood off his head. A huge Ferris wheel became visible in the distance through the rainy night. A man was outlined against the Ferris wheel. He wore a fedora and a trench coat, lowering an umbrella as he came toward Tree. Dahlia stepped forward and rather formally embraced him. He said something to her in what sounded like Russian. She turned and nodded to the two Russian friends flanking Tree. The taller friend pressed a pistol against Tree's ear.

"Perhaps you should introduce us, Dahlia," said the man in the trench coat.

"I believe you have already spoken to each other on the phone," Dahlia said.

"Volkova." Tree couldn't help making the name sound ominous.

"And you must be the irksome Tree Callister." Volkova made Tree's name sound much less ominous.

"Why is this man holding a gun to my head?"

"So that he is prepared if I decide you should be shot," replied Volkova reasonably.

"What would make you decide to do that?" Tree was having trouble breathing.

"If you do not pass my little test."

"Test?" Tree asked nervously. "What kind of test?"

"Do you fancy yourself as something of a film…what do they call it? A film *buff?*"

Tree looked at Volkova trying to figure out where this was headed. "Yeah, I suppose I am," he answered carefully. "What difference does it make?"

"A great deal of difference to me," Volkova stated. "It will make a great deal of difference to you too should you fail to answer correctly."

Tree couldn't believe what he was hearing. But then it was hard to keep track of all the unbelievable things he had heard lately.

"You're on hallowed cinematic ground," Volkova was saying. "Why is that?"

"I am unfamiliar with Vienna," Tree said.

"But you have been to the movies—or so you say."

Tree took a deep breath, taking in his surroundings, the big Ferris wheel outlined in lights through the mist and rain.

It hit him suddenly where he was. Hallowed cinematic ground indeed. He had been here before.

"We're in the Prater," Tree announced, perhaps louder than necessary. "*The Third Man* was filmed here." He pointed to the gigantic Ferris wheel "That's the famous Prater wheel where Orson Welles made one of the most famous speeches in film history…"

"'In Italy, for thirty years under the Borgias,'" intoned Volkova, "'they had warfare, terror, murder, and bloodshed…'"

"'And they produced Michelangelo, Leonardo da Vinci and the Renaissance,'" continued Tree. "'In Switzerland, they had five hundred years of brotherly love and five hundred years of democracy, and what did that produce?'"

"'The cuckoo clock!'" Volkova finished with great satisfaction. "Well done, my friend." As though to demonstrate friendship he nodded to the man with the gun. It was promptly taken away from Tree's head. Dahlia appeared almost as relieved as Tree.

"*The Third Man* is my most favorite movie," Volkova went on. "I recite what is called The Cuckoo Clock Speech to myself every so often as a reminder of its basic truth."

"And that is?"

"Chaos works. Chaos in the end produces the best outcomes. Chaos tests us; it requires strength and innovation to overcome it. Chaos defeats your opponents."

"Is that why we're standing here in the rain? Demonstrating the strength of chaos?"

"*My* strength, Tree Callister. I wanted you to understand how easy it would be to kill you, how powerless your so-called friends are, the American agents who have lied to you and brought you here under the illusion that if you cooperate with them you will get your wife back and everything would end happily, as in all those infantile Hollywood movies."

"I don't know anything about American agents," Tree said, feeling as though he was on firmer ground without a gun at his head.

"The CIA thinks that by bringing you here, they could trap me. That is their intention. They are so stupid. It's not going to happen."

"You told me to come to Vienna with the tiara," Tree said insistently. "I'm in Vienna. I have the tiara. I even answered your skill-testing question. Now where is my wife?"

Volkova lowered his umbrella and came forward with a pitying look an instant before he punched tree hard in the gut. Tree sagged to the ground. Down on his knees, he couldn't stop Volkova delivering a kick that knocked him onto his side. Tree vaguely heard Dahlia say, "That's enough, Boris."

"Shut up," Volkova replied.

Tree lay wheezing on the wet pavement as Volkova stood over him. "You have made a grave mistake, Tree Callister. You have brought the cavalry with you, people so dumb they thought that I could be deceived. Get rid of them. Deliver the tiara to me. Do not try to betray me again. If you do, you will never see your wife. She will be dead and so will you."

He bent down quickly and dropped a cell phone close to Tree's face. "Do not use any phone they have supplied you with. Use only this phone." Footsteps soon faded away. There was only the sound of rain splattering against the pavement.

And Tree groaning.

34

The rain stopped. Tree stirred on the pavement. One of these days, he decided, he would get to his feet. He would attempt to do that. He couldn't lay on the stones of Vienna forever, everything in his body once again hurting, could he? Part of him swore there was no reason in the world why he couldn't. He rolled onto his back so that he had a view of the Prater wheel. There was a clear night sky. A full moon hung over the wheel. The moon aglow, the wheel outlined in light. He thought of Orson Welles revealing himself to a naïve Joseph Cotten in *The Third Man*. He thought of what a patsy was Holly Martins, the Cotten character, failing to understand Harry Lime's criminality until it was almost too late. Was he that same kind of patsy? The ghost of Holly Martins was with him in this park.

He got onto his knees and picked up the phone that Volkova had left beside him and then pulled himself to his feet. A bravura achievement, he decided, one he'd had to perform far too often lately due to the fact that people kept beating the shit out of him. Holly Martins as a punching bag.

He gazed around, turning his face to the wind. A stray newspaper whipped past him. What do you know, he thought, they still produce newspapers in Vienna.

He patted his jacket pocket discovering that he still had his billfold they had supplied him with before he left Florida. It contained his passport, an American Express credit card, and one thousand Euros in cash. He began to feel stronger. The gut pain resulting from Volkova's punch had dissipated.

He made his way out of the park and reached a rain-slicked avenue. He was caught momentarily in the glare of oncoming headlights. Then the lights were gone. He was alone in the windswept dark, feeling very much alone in a city about which he knew nothing, except it stood as the black-and-white, war-torn background for the movie whose love he shared with the Russian agent threatening to kill him and his wife. He could not go back to the Sacher, he decided. Judy and the CIA were at the Sacher. Volkova had blown their cover. From now on, he had to go it alone. The question was, how do you go it alone when you're lost?

A truck passed illuminating a side street. Not knowing what else to do, he turned down it, feeling as if he was descending into an unmapped underworld, which, in a way he was. The street fed into a square. A light blazed over a small hotel on the corner.

Reaching the entrance, he found the doors locked. He pressed an intercom on the wall. There was a buzz and the door clicked open. Inside the tiny lobby, the woman behind a desk cluttered with tourist brochures advertising the sights of Vienna, gave him a startled look, taking in his bedraggled state. Thankfully, she spoke English. Tree babbled something about a fight with his wife and had how he come through the rain in search of a place to stay the night.

The clerk could have cared less. Whatever his problem, it was his problem, the best she could do was offer him a room.

He paid the required euros and presented his passport. She handed him an old-fashioned brass key attached to a wooden plaque with 307 printed on it. The lift was out of order, advised the clerk. Guests would have to use the stairs.

Tree started up a narrow, winding staircase, a challenge that reignited all the aches he had collected recently. He reached

307—a room approximately the size of a closet—and collapsed on the double bed. He told himself, he could not close his eyes, he had to think about what to do next. He had to come up with something. He could think of nothing.

He was asleep almost immediately.

The Orange Man did not come.

After all, Tree was asleep in an anonymous hotel on an anonymous street in a city he did not know. If Tree had no idea where he was, how could the Orange Man find him?

He blinked his eyes open. Morning sunlight seeped through the curtains of his closet-like room. He could hear voices in the hall outside. For an instant, he feared Volkova was coming for him. But the voices soon disappeared. He was safe for the moment. He managed to sit up, realizing he had fallen asleep in his wet clothes. He got unsteadily to his feet and slowly undressed.

The hand-held shower provided a weak spray of hot water that managed to more or less do the job of reviving him, and give momentary relief to aching limbs. From the other room, came the shrill blast of the house phone. When he picked up the receiver, a tired voice said, "This is the front desk. There is a package here for you."

"For me? Are you sure?"

"Are you not Herr Callister?"

"Yes," Tree said.

"Then this package is for you."

Confused and frightened, Tree dressed quickly. How could anyone possibly know where he was? He barely knew himself. The lift still wasn't working. He limped down the stairs. The package, wrapped in brown paper, sat on the front desk, eyed suspiciously by the elderly clerk who was now on the desk. In a city like Vienna, it was wise to be wary of unidentified packages.

As soon as Tree picked up the package the clerk looked relieved. If it went off it would blow up Tree, not him. There was an alcove off the lobby where they were serving the breakfast that went with the room. A gray-haired couple, both wearing shorts, a map of Vienna spread out across their small table, nodded to him. They watched him curiously, reminding him that in his damp, muddy clothes he must look like hell.

Back in his room, he laid the package on the bed. He tore off the brown wrapping paper, exposing a white cardboard box. He opened the lid.

The Alexandra Tiara lay on a bed of scrunched-up newspapers.

When Tree phoned the front desk, the clerk sounded annoyed that he was once again being bothered. However, he readily agreed to send someone to collect Tree's clothes and get them laundered. The maid who arrived a few minutes later, accepted them through a partially open door and in good English promised to have everything back by six o'clock.

Tree lay on his bed, the cell phone at his side. He felt much better when he was lying down. He closed his eyes. The next thing he knew, the phone started vibrating. He sat up groggily. The room was in shadow. He reached for the phone. "Do you have it?" the voice asked.

Tree looked at the tiara beside him on the bed. "Yes," he said. "I do."

"The park behind the Belvedere at 10 o'clock," the voice said. "If you do not come alone, if you bring anyone, we will kill your wife."

The line went dead.

35

He found a laundry bag in the closet and placed the tiara in it. The lift was finally back in operation and so he took it down to the lobby. The same woman who had been on the desk when he checked in treated him to the same doubting look despite the fact he had cleaned himself up. She explained that the Belvedere he was asking about was the Belvedere Museum, notable because it housed the few Klimt paintings not in the hands of private owners. She ordered a taxi for him.

Fifteen minutes later, his taxi drew to a stop in front of the grandly ornate ivory facade of the former Belvedere Palace, the Upper Belvedere, the driver informed him. He paused to take in the palace's decorative stonework, the sculptures, the endless windows and pilasters. For all its magnificence, Tree could not imagine how anyone could actually live there.

There was an enormous set of stairs to be climbed. Tree felt as though any onlookers were being exposed to a view of a crippled old guy carrying a laundry bag, barely able to reach the top. Pausing to catch his breath and give his aching limbs a rest, Tree speculated about what kind of stamina the Hapsburg royalty must have had in order to always be climbing countless steps. He started out again, making his way through a series of terraces and gardens to the rear of the palace. In the gathering dusk, a vast plain of formal grounds spread before him, intersected by ornate fountains.

Somewhere down there, he thought, Boris Volkova waited with Freddie. He did not want to think about how the tiara he carried had arrived at his hotel. He had it and that was all that mattered. He didn't care about anything else, not about who was conspiring against who, none of it made any difference. As long as he got Freddie back.

Darkness fell over the park. The sky turned a deep purple filled with stars. Tree moved down past a winged sphinx on marble haunches and then along with one of the pathways. He had no idea where he should go, growing increasingly anxious as the ten o'clock hour drew closer. He reached one of the baroque fountains. In the distance, he could hear music. Someone was having a good time, he mused. Not him. Not tonight.

Boris Volkova appeared suddenly in the moonlight, drawing a grunt of surprise from Tree. He stepped back as Volkova came toward him, staying away from another sucker punch. Volkova pointed to the bag Tree was carrying. "Is that it?"

"Where's my wife?' Tree demanded.

"Give it to me," Volkova ordered.

Tree managed to call out, "You agreed that Freddie—" before he was knocked to the ground from behind. Volkova immediately bent down and grabbed the bag out of Tree's hand. Down on his knees, Tree became aware of the hulking presence of the three men accompanying Volkova. Tree lifted his head enough so that he could see Volkova open the bag and check inside. Apparently satisfied, the Russian turned and started away, followed by his men. Tree screamed after them as he got to his feet. The next thing, Dahlia was beside him, taking his arm.

He gaped at her incredulously, his mind a blur of questions. He barely heard her say, "We have to go, there's no time."

"Go? Go where?"

"Come with me," she said. Her hand tightening on his arm directing him away from the fountain. As they moved off, Tree glanced around. Volkova had disappeared with the tiara.

He was left empty-handed and there was no sign of Freddie. Crushed, he allowed Dahlia to guide him to the line of trees bordering the park. They went through and down onto the street where a black Mercedes sedan was parked. When they got to the sidewalk, she pressed a key fob into his hand.

"Drive," she breathed. "Get the hell out of here."

"What's going on?" he asked in a choked voice, barely holding in check his growing sense of panic. "Whose side are you on?"

"I'm on the side that pays me the most," she said. "Right now, that's the side that wants me to make sure you're safely away from here. Quit asking questions, get in the car."

He went into the street and opened the driver's-side door and got in. The figure in the passenger seat was all but lost in deep shadows.

"Darling," Freddie Stayner said, catching the light as she leaned into him.

36

They embraced with a tentativeness as though neither of them could quite believe they were together. But they were. This was Freddie, in his arms again. He couldn't hold back tears. Neither could she.

"How—" he started to ask.

"I don't know. This is so..." Freddie for a moment was at a loss for words. There were more tears until she found them: "...God, Tree, so unexpected..." She quickly gathered herself together. "But right now, darling, we must get away. We can talk later once it's safe."

They still weren't safe? Of course not. How in this dangerous world they continued to be lost in, could they possibly be safe? Tree started the engine and swung onto the roadway. He picked up speed. Freddie clung to him. "Do you have any idea where we're going?" she asked.

"Not a clue," Tree said.

She leaned back for a better view of him in the light from the occasional oncoming vehicle. "You look terrible," she said worriedly. She reached out to touch gently at his face. "What have you done to yourself?"

"It's not me," Tree said. "It's the people who didn't want me to find you who keep beating me up."

"You wanted me—which is wonderful; they wanted the tiara, not so wonderful," Freddie pointed out.

"Now I've got you back and Volkova has the tiara—or more to the point Vladimir Putin has it."

"But how did all this happen?" Freddie asked.

"Okay, I'm doing a lot of guessing here, but I think we are pawns in a game the CIA, in partnership with the FBI, is playing in order to make sure that Putin gets his tiara."

"But why would they need us to accomplish that?'

"To hide the fact that the CIA is behind the whole thing. This all got started when Judy learned that the only way to remain a friend of Vlady's was to give him what he so badly wanted,

The Alexandra Tiara. I can't be sure, but because of Judy's suspect business activities with Russia, the FBI was already investigating her. When they discovered what was happening, they forced her into cooperating with them."

"But what does any of that accomplish—except Putin now has his tiara."

"I don't know," Tree said. "Volkova thought they were after him, but I'm not so sure. Last night, I was finished. I was either going to deliver the tiara or Volkova was going to make sure we both ended up dead."

"But you had the tiara when you came to the park," Freddie pointed out.

"That's the thing. No one could have known where I was staying—I barely knew myself. But somehow a package was delivered this morning. Inside was the tiara."

"They knew."

"I must have been followed from the Sacher. They knew where I was all along, but they were careful to make it appear as though I was acting alone."

"What about Dahlia?" Freddie asked. "She got me away from Volkova and arranged for our escape."

"Whoever pays, that's the side that Dahlia is on. The CIA must have paid up."

"I was totally in the dark," Freddie said. "Actually, I was

oblivious from the moment Volkova's agents pulled me out of the wreck of our car."

"After they ran us off the road."

"I ended up in Moscow with no idea how or why I got there. Boris Volkova seemed to be in charge, Putin's puppet as far as I could make out. He was determined to do what it took to get that tiara for his boss—kill me if it was necessary. Kill anyone who got in his way—including Gladys, I think."

"How were you treated?" Tree asked.

"Not so bad, I guess. I mean they didn't poison me or ship me off to the Gulag. They held me at what I was told was a dacha in a Moscow suburb. Volkova kept reassuring me that if everyone did what they were supposed to do, I would get home safely. Even so, I was beginning to doubt I would ever see you again when out of nowhere I was flown to what I learned was Vienna and then held in one of their safe houses."

"Why we must get as far away as we can," Tree said, "away from everyone who's involved in this mess."

"What are you suggesting?"

"What do you say we drive to Paris? Once we're there, we can catch a breath and figure out next steps."

"Do you know how to get to Paris?" asked Freddie.

Tree pointed to the dashboard screen. "GPS can get us there."

"Are you sure you're up for this, Tree? You look pretty banged up."

"We can spell each other off on the drive," Tree countered. "If I'm with you, I can accomplish anything."

"What about money? Do we have any?"

"Cash and a credit card, courtesy of my pals at the CIA."

"Paris," Freddie said, hugging against him. "Why not? We'll fool them all. Let's do it."

37

The GPS guided the Mercedes along the A4 through Germany and into France. They arrived in Paris thirteen hours later. The Hotel Regina, opposite the Louvre, offered the old-world comfort and charm that was part of the fantasy Paris they both loved. Audrey Hepburn would have been comfortable in their high-ceilinged room. Freddie and Tree showered and then, swathed in the hotel's fluffy white robes, fell into bed.

Arms enveloped him. Tree's eyes sprang open in alarm. Freddie pressed herself against him, holding him tight. "It's all right, Tree, you're with me," she murmured. "It's all going to be fine. I love you…"

"I love you too," he returned. "Love you so much." Feeling warm and safe, holding onto her for dear life, overcome with emotion.

They made love. How could they not in a magnificent Paris hotel room fit for Audrey Hepburn? The sheer joy of the two of them experiencing each other after such a forced abstinence reminding themselves how much they needed one another, and how wondrous and all-consuming was that need.

Then, predictably, they were hungry. Starving. Unable to remember the last time either of them had had a decent meal. This was Paris after all, the world capital of decent meals.

"It means rousing ourselves to get dressed," Freddie pointed out.

"We could order room service."

Freddie made a face. "Should one ever order room service when one is in Paris?"

"When two people have been through what we have been through, room service looks like a pretty good option," Tree said.

"I've a better idea." Freddie nuzzled against him.

"You always do," he said.

"La Closerie des Lilas on Boulevard du Montparnasse. You took me there the first time we were in Paris together. That was the night I decided there was more to you than your rather sketchy reputation as a Chicago newspaper reporter suggested."

"Highly exaggerated," Tree argued.

"I'm not so sure about that," Freddie countered. "Even so that night at La Closerie des Lilas changed my mind about you." She kissed him. "Of course, I had no idea what I was getting myself into."

"Any regrets?" Tree asked.

"None at all," Freddie said. "As long as you take me to the Closerie for dinner."

"Then how could I say no?"

"You can't." She kissed him some more.

Before he met Freddie, Tree hung out at La Closerie des Lilas when he was in town for work, mostly because Hemingway had frequented the place in the 1920s. Hemingway had written about it in his memoir of Paris, *A Moveable Feast*, and there was a plaque at the end of the bar where he was supposed to have sat.

Tonight, there were no thoughts of Hemingway, only Freddie so beautiful in the golden light of the brasserie, the pianist adding to the romantic atmosphere with his version of "The Way You Look Tonight." As always, escargots for him, the foie gras for her. The pain, the horrors they had both endured, all gone in the joy of being back at one of their favorite haunts— the joy of each other. Forever...

Except forever, as it always is, was fleeting.

Travis Dunn of the CIA took his time drawing up an empty chair before joining them. He was in the beautifully tailored navy suit that he had been born to inhabit. "This is quite ironic," he said cheerfully. "As it happens La Closerie des Lilas is one of my favorite Paris brasseries. It's not as well-known as some of the other Hemingway haunts like Les Deux Magots and Le Select, but I suppose that's what makes it so much more special."

All Tree could do was stare, speechless. Freddie was shaking her head in confusion. "Who is this?"

"Mr. Travis Dunn is with the Central Intelligence Agency," Tree said, finding his voice.

"I must say you threw us off a bit getting out of Vienna as fast as you did," Dunn offered, "Not for long though. The tracking device attached to your car did what it was supposed to do and so here we are this evening."

Dunn sat back in his chair, apparently satisfied with the effect he was having on Freddie and Tree. "Personally," he continued, "I'm happy we're meeting in Paris. I know one is supposed to fall in love with Vienna, and I suppose if you love schnitzel and can't wait to taste the torte at the Sacher, it's for you. But since I don't like schnitzel and the torte is far too bitter for my taste—"

"Dunn, stop it. What the hell are you doing here," Tree interrupted. "What's this all about?"

The CIA agent appeared unfazed by Tree's outburst. "Yes,

you're right. My apologies. And apologies for interrupting what looks like a lovely dinner—given what you have been through, I can imagine a night like this is what you both need. But I thought I'd better drop by to ask how you plan to get back to the good old U.S. of A."

"Why would that be any concern of yours?" demanded a peeved Freddie.

Dunn reached into his inside coat pocket and drew out two envelopes. He placed one of them in front of Tree. The other was for Freddie. "Two passports. First class airline tickets. A few euros for expenses."

"Why?" Tree asked.

Dunn tapped the envelope in front of Tree with his forefinger for emphasis. "Call it payment for your silence."

"You don't want us talking about the Alexandra Tiara, is that it?" Freddie said accusatorially.

"I understand that you have plans to leave Florida," Dunn said, apparently sidestepping the question. "That's a very good idea. Put all of this behind you. A fresh start."

"I don't understand why you've gone to so much trouble," Tree said.

"Trouble that almost got my husband killed," Freddie added.

"That was the most unfortunate aspect of the whole thing," Dunn said. "I must say, Tree, you came through with flying colors. I think it's safe to say you surprised us all."

"You obviously don't know my husband." Freddie took Tree's hand. "No one ever thinks he can come through, but then he always does." She gazed at Tree with shining eyes. "He's quite a guy."

"I have the most remarkable wife," Tree said. "She's put up with a lot." He focused on Dunn. "I know you and the FBI were out to destroy Legio Three and the crazies behind it, but I suspect you could have done it without the tiara."

"Maybe so," Dunn conceded, "For the sake of argument, let's say we wanted to ensure that President Putin got what he wanted to get."

"Volkova thought you were after him."

"Obviously, that wasn't the case," Dunn replied.

"Then what?" Freddie asked in amazement. "None of it makes make any sense."

"In this business, many things don't make sense," Dunn said. "At least not at first."

"Then all this will somehow make sense at some future date, is that what you're saying?"

"We will see." Dunn offered.

"What about Judy?" Tree asked. "Is she going to prison?"

"Your ex-wife," Dunn said needlessly. "You two have had quite the history together."

"That's an understatement if I ever heard one," Freddie observed.

"She hasn't exactly been an ally in all this, has she?" Dunn said to Tree.

"With Judy, it's always hard to say," Tree acknowledged. "The same goes, I imagine, for Red Dahlia."

"Although her alliances can be fleeting, Dahlia has decided that she is not so red after all given the current climate and is better off working for us," Dunn said. "The same holds true for Mrs. Markov."

"But is she going to prison?" Freddie pressed.

"I would say that for now, Mrs. Markov is more helpful to us outside prison than she is in."

"Apparently, there is much to look forward to in the future," Freddie said wryly.

"Isn't that the way with the future?" Dunn said ambiguously. He glanced at his watch, and then at their empty dishes. "It looks as though you've finished with your starters. I do love the escargots here. I'm afraid, though, there won't be time for main courses this evening. There's a car waiting for you outside that will take you to Charles De Gaulle airport."

Freddie and Tree exchanged glances. She glared at Dunn. "We've only just met but already I've decided you are a bastard."

"And if Freddie decides you're a bastard, well, that's it," Tree acknowledged. "You're a bastard."

"How could a man who drags two lovers out of one of Paris's most romantic restaurants be anything else?" Dunn acknowledged. "But we'd better get you going. Otherwise, you'll miss your plane. Don't worry about the bill. I'll take care of it. In fact, I may stay behind and have some of those delicious escargots."

38

The loud clang of a steel door made Tree refocus as he followed the portly guard along a dark, airless corridor. An angry voice could be heard. Someone shouted for the angry voice to shut up. The angry voice grew angrier.

The guard stopped and opened a door. "You got fifteen minutes," he said. Tree stepped across the threshold into a small badly lit room containing a table and two chairs. Almost as soon as he took a seat, another door opened and the Orange Man, escorted by a youthful guard, entered. He wore, appropriately enough, an orange jumpsuit. His hands were handcuffed in front of him. He looked pale and bloated and not happy to see Tree.

"It's not what you think," he insisted as the guard got him seated.

"What should I think?" Tree asked.

"I'm a political prisoner held by a deep state out to silence me."

"I guess I should have known that's how you'd rationalize this," Tree said.

"And don't start thinking you've won," the Orange Man sneered.

"No? Funny, I've got my wife back, not to mention my life, and here you are behind bars, wearing handcuffs and an orange jumpsuit. You're not looking much like a winner."

"Don't kid yourself, I always win," declared the Orange Man. "I don't go away. People like me, we will always rise again. This is a momentary setback. In the end, I come out on top. Guys like you, Tree, nice guys, guys who stumble around trying to do what you think is the right thing, you always lose. Sometimes, like now, you think you've won, but that's a joke."

Tree got to his feet.

The Orange Man looked uncustomarily troubled. "Wait a minute. Where are you going?"

"I'm walking out of here. I can do that," Tree said. "You're not going to haunt me anymore. I'm free of you, free of everything that has stopped me from getting on with my life."

The Orange Man was on his feet. His blubbery face had turned beet red. "You're a loser. You stick with me, I'm a winner."

"No, you're not, it's all an illusion. I've spent most of my life thinking I was a fraud, a bad actor on a stage I don't know how to cross," Tree said. "But you know what? I've done pretty well for myself. A whole lot better than you. You're the loser."

Tree started for the door.

"You bastard, I'm a winner!" Tree heard the Orange Man say. As Tree reached the door and started to open it, the Orange Man pounced. His arms somehow were around Tree's neck. The chain between the handcuffs pressed against his throat. "I'm doing what all those people over the years couldn't do," the Orange Man hissed into Tree's ear. "I'm killing you!"

"No," Tree shouted out as the chain dug into his throat. "Help! He's trying to kill me!"

Tree couldn't breathe. Blood gushed from his throat. The ugly determined grunts from the Orange Man filled the room. "Die, you bastard—*die!*"

Everything went black.

Freddie found Tree on the edge of the bed, taking deep

breaths. "It was the Orange Man," he announced. "He just killed me."

"The Orange Man?"

"Every time I fell asleep lately, he's been there, calling me names, making my life hell."

"I'm sure you're not going to believe anything your Orange Man has to say," she said sympathetically.

"But then he killed me. This was after he slept with you."

"Except, you're very much alive." Freddie spoke with infinite reasonableness. "And he certainly never slept with me. Honestly, you and your silly dreams."

Yes, he thought. Freddie was right. Freddie was always right.

"Come along and get dressed," she said. "It's time to say goodbye to a life."

One last time they crossed the jerry-rigged causeway to Sanibel Island. There was talk of building a more permanent structure, but thus far only talk. There was a lot of talk about a lot of things on Sanibel but the reality was that there were still hundreds of condominiums without power, businesses and resorts unable to reopen, insurance companies that weren't paying, visitors who had yet to return and who had no place to stay if they did.

"How are you feeling?" Freddie asked as they exited the causeway.

"I'm not sure," Tree answered. "Caught somewhere between nostalgia and regret, I suppose."

"Regret?"

"That I couldn't have done a lot of things better, that I didn't protect us more. Trying to figure out how I ever got into stuff I had no intention of getting into and then not knowing how to get out again."

"Or from my perspective, discovering that you actually liked the trouble, enjoyed the danger," Freddie said. "It gave you a sense of yourself that you liked. This idea that you were a resourceful tough guy. And you know what," she added, "it turned out that you *were* a pretty resourceful tough guy."

"Not that tough, I'm afraid," Tree said.

"Tough enough. No one was more surprised than you were," Freddie continued. "You gave lip service to wanting out of all that, without really trying very hard to do it."

"Whatever the truth of all that, whatever it was driving me, that's all gone," Tree said. "It's as though the spell has been broken."

"Are you sure about that? I've heard this many, many times— usually just before you go off and get into more trouble."

"This really is the Sanibel Sunset Detective's last case," Tree said insistently. "Helped by the fact that we're leaving the scene of my many crimes."

They were interrupted by the sound of Tree's phone. "Where are you?" Rex Baxter's voice on the speaker filled the car."

"We're coming onto Sanibel for the last time," Tree said.

"Tree has informed me that this is his last case," Freddie added.

"Yeah, well, we'll see about that," Rex replied caustically.

"How are you doing, Rex?" Freddie asked.

"Never better out here in La La Land. You'll never guess who I'm having lunch with at the Beverly Wilshire Hotel."

"Hello, Tree." The unmistakable voice of Judy Markov. The unnaturally joyful voice of Judy Markov.

"Judy?" Tree said in astonishment.

"We thought you were in prison," said Freddie.

"No, I'm in Hollywood," Judy said. "Depending on your point of view, I suppose it could be the same thing, only with palm trees and swimming pools."

"We're celebrating the fact that Judy has sold her book to MGM, for six figures, as they say out here," put in Rex.

"You've written a *book*?"

"I've written *part* of a book," Judy amended. "Enough to interest a publisher and now a Hollywood movie studio."

"You've gotta admit, Judy's had quite a life," Rex said.

A life that included far too much of him, Tree mused.

"*American Oligarch*, that's the title they've come up with. Thanks to you, Tree," she went on triumphantly, "it looks as though I'm going to be rich again. Not as rich as I was before, of course, but I'll take it."

"Tree, you've made us both rich," chimed in Rex.

"It looks like our lunch has arrived," Judy said. "We will talk more later."

Tree wanted to assure her it wasn't necessary to talk further, but then Rex said, "Good luck, you two. I'll see you soon in Chicago."

Tree started to say he and Freddie were passing by the white clapboard building where the Sanibel-Captiva Chamber of Commerce was headquartered and where Tree had started out as a private detective, but by then Rex was gone. Freddie leaned over and gave him a hug. "We're rich in so many other ways," she said.

Lucky for him, Tree reflected. His first client—his only client at the time—had been a twelve-year-old named Marcello. He had hired Tree for the princely sum of twelve dollars to find his mother. He found the mother but Marcello never paid the twelve dollars.

He'd had a lot of clients like that. Nearly getting killed any number of times over the years was not a high-paying gig.

But that was okay. He had managed to stay alive and married to Freddie and that was reward enough.

In sad silence they drove through the no-man's land of San Cap Road. They mourned the loss of their house on Andy Rosse Lane. Tree felt his emotions begin to bubble uncontrollably to the surface. He cleared his throat and swallowed hard. At the end of the street, they parked at the Mucky Duck and then walked to the beach.

Ordinarily, crowds of tourists watched the sun set over the Gulf of Mexico. For years Freddie and Tree had listened from their terrace to the cries and gasps of pleasure as dusk fell and all, for a moment, was well with the world. Today, they were alone, save for a few stragglers along the shoreline. The sun was nearly lost in colors red and gold. Freddie leaned against Tree. "I love you," she said. "You are my knight in shining armor."

"Slightly tarnished," Tree said.

"But you came for me. 'Strong in will to strive, to seek, to find, and not to yield'—that's you."

"Wow," said Tree. "Where did that come from?"

"Tennyson," Freddie replied. "Alfred Lord."

"Well, I had to find you," he said. "You're my life. Everything. Without you—" he began to well up. He could barely finish. "Without you …there's nothing…"

"Hey," she said. "Detectives don't cry."

"I'm not a detective anymore," Tree said. Tears rolled down his face. The sun sank unceremoniously out of sight. He took her in his arms. Now there were tears in her eyes as she looked up at him. "It's time," she said.

Tree nodded and said, "Let's go home, Freddie."

Epilogue

Putin Is Safe After Assassination Attempt

MOSCOW (AP)— Russian president Vladimir V. Putin has narrowly survived an assassination attempt.

Details are scarce, but Russian state media reported that an explosive device may have been planted in a jewel-encrusted tiara that once belonged to Czarina Alexandra Feodorovna, the last Empress of Russia. President Putin has long campaigned for the return of the tiara that for years was thought to be lost following the execution of Alexandra and her husband, Nicholas II, and their five children.

Mr. Putin's spokesman, Dmitri S. Peskov, said the Russian president had suffered only minor injuries and had been released from hospital. However, Boris Volkova, known to be one of Putin's closest confidants, was killed when the device exploded. Two of Mr. Putin's security guards were wounded. They are recovering in hospital.

Mr. Peskov in a statement accused the Central Intelligence Agency of being behind the assassination attempt. "This was a carefully orchestrated plot hatched by American agents," Mr. Peskov said. He went on to accuse Ukrainian intelligence of collaborating with the CIA in order to kill President Putin.

A Ukrainian Foreign Ministry official denied that his country played any role in the assassination attempt.

A source in Russian state security who did not want to be named, said that the tiara was rigged with an explosive device that could be remotely detonated. He said the tiara had been returned to a Russian official in Vienna and from there was transported to Moscow.

President Putin was in his office when the tiara arrived, sources said, but had stepped out moments before it exploded.

In Washington, a state department spokesman denied that the United States had any involvement in the assassination attempt. "That's ridiculous," said Austin Kirby, "we are not in the business of trying to kill anyone, no matter how odious."

The attempt on President Putin's life came as the Justice Department issued indictments for members of a secretive right-wing group headquartered in Sarasota, Florida. The DOJ said the group was mixed up in a series of murders in Weeki Wachee and Sarasota associated with the tiara. FBI agents arrested Matthew "Buck" Ares, who heads an organization called Legio Three. Mr. Ayres refers to the group as "my army," and calls himself its general.

Also arrested was Damian Fargo who goes by the name Orcus, and his stepmother, Alina Kozlov. The two are said to have financed the Legio Three organization over the years. The defendants are facing various murder and espionage charges.

"The defendants were part of what presented itself as a right-wing organization dedicated to protecting conservative American values," said Assistant Attorney General Kristen Clarke. "But in fact, they basically acted as a murderous American arm of Russian intelligence known as the Oprichnik, reporting directly to Vladimir Putin.

Ms. Clarke said that the defendants conspired to commit at least three murders in their efforts to obtain the Alexandra Tiara for President Putin.

Lawyers for the defendants maintained that their clients are innocent. "These are law-bidding citizens who have done nothing wrong," said defense lawyer Ilina A. Isav. "They are being persecuted by a liberal justice department simply because they espouse conservative views. There is nothing more to it than that. This is a travesty of justice."

Acknowledgements

My brother Ric introduced me to Sanibel and Captiva Islands. He suggested I write something set there. "Whatever you do," he advised, "make sure Sanibel is in the title." I did and the Sanibel Sunset Detective was born. My life was forever changed. Not content with rescuing my fading career, Ric took over production of the books. At the same time, he used his many connections to introduce me and Tree Callister around the islands.

For nearly twenty years and almost as many books, ours has been a wonderful collaboration. As I have said so many times, I couldn't have done any of it without him.

Equally, the Sanibel Sunset Detective could never have lived without the love and support of my wife, Kathy. Not only is she the indispensable first reader of these novels, but thanks to her, we found a place in Fort Myers, not far from Sanibel. With a new novel in tow, we came to Florida each year to take up residence at our Gulf Harbour condo. This became our routine—the change in our lives that neither of us had expected but which we enjoyed immensely.

I thought we would go on like this forever. The pandemic and Hurricane Ian were sharp reminders that forever has limits. Ian in particular swept away just about everything Ric and I had spent years building up.

Like Tree and Freddie in the novel, Kathy and I decided it was time to move on. Age might also have had something to do with our decision. The Sanibel Sunset Detective is more or less ageless. His creator would like to think so too, but damnable reality keeps intruding. The heart was no longer into the constant book signings and promotions and neither was the body.

Tree Callister, however, couldn't leave without getting mixed up in one more adventure. As always, getting down the particulars of the Sanibel Sunset Detective's last case has been very much a team effort. In addition to Ric and Kathy, a number of people once again saved me from myself. James Bryan Simpson was back with his eagle eye and sharp pencil. My old pal, Ray Bennett, who has worked on so many books with me, weighed in from his new digs outside London.

Special thanks go to Stephen Froom, longtime editor and a fan of the books. In addition to working with his son Mitchell Froom to produce the first Sanibel Sunset Detective audio book, narrated by Stephen, he did excellent work on the final edit. Also, many thanks to longtime friend and designer, Jennifer Smith, who brought patience and creativity to the book's cover.

Many people have helped keep the books alive over the past two decades. The late and much missed Brian Vallee (my dear friend who created West-End Books and got this whole venture started), David Kendall (who improved so many of my novels), my sisters-in-law Alexandra Lenhoff and Alicia Base, Joel Ruddy, Erin Ruddy, Lindsay Base, Eric Base, Bob Burt, Kim Hunter (who chauffeured the author to Florida in his pickup truck), Bridgit Stone-Budd (the first covers were her creations), Scott and Candy Thompson, Susie Holly (sharp-eyed editor of all things Sanibel), Hollie Schmid, Richard Johnson, Gene Massey, Rebecca Binkowski, Annette Stillson, Rodney Wade, Rick Winningham, Duane Shaffer, Josh Stewart, Mickey Ferry, Kathy Kozar-Parsley, Pete and Shelley Cervone, Stephen Peach, Jennifer Schiff, Christine Lemmon.

Finally, and most importantly, heartfelt appreciation to the thousands of readers who have so enthusiastically embraced the novels. Meeting, and in many cases becoming friends with the people who read the books, has been the greatest pleasure of this entire experience. I have laughed with readers, cried on occasion, hugged them, and listened to their funny, moving, and sometimes incredible stories. What I will miss most as I say goodbye to the Sanibel Sunset Detective, is you, the wonderful reader.

Already, several of you have asked if this is really the Sanibel Sunset Detective's last case. Certainly, Freddie and Rex Baxter are not convinced. Tree Callister, on the other hand, swears this is the end.

We shall see…

Contact Ron Base
baseron2001@gmail.com

Meet Priscilla Tempest
The plucky Heroine of Ron Base's latest mystery series

Priscilla heads the press office at the iconic Savoy Hotel in
1968, the era of Swinging London, sex scandals, tough gang-
sters, crooked politicians and duplicitous royals. Priscilla tries
her best to stay out of trouble, but she can never quite do it.
Her adventures (co-written with Prudence Emery) have been
published so far in three novels: *Death at the Savoy*, *Scandal at
the Savoy*, and *Princess of the Savoy*.
   The fourth novel in the series is titled
Curse of the Savoy.
Read an excerpt from the latest Priscilla Tempest mystery...

The Dinner Party

The notorious dinner that triggered the curse was held in the Savoy Hotel's Pinafore Room. It was hosted by the legendary American filmmaker and actor, Orson Welles, who was adamant that his guests enjoy the very best that the Savoy could offer.

In pursuit of excellence, Welles had worked tirelessly with Paolo Contarini, the hotel's banquet manager. The rhododendrons and azaleas were flown in from the Riviera. The pale-pink tablecloth was of the finest Irish linen, excellent for showing off the china. The Chablis Grand Crû came directly from the Savoy's cavernous wine cellars.

A shame, then, that the curse overwhelmed everything. Or did it? There followed blackmail and murder, certainly, as well as a ruthless effort to cover up foul deeds. But was that because of the curse? Or was the series of terrible events that subsequently unfolded and which nearly got Miss Priscilla Tempest killed, mere coincidence? In London's highest levels of society, among the very few in possession of at least part of the story, there was considerable debate.

And then there were the whispers about how the Queen of England became involved.

But we begin with that infamous dinner...

Fourteen guests, impressive in their various levels of notoriety, had been invited. In addition to Welles, they were the film director Alfred Hitchcock; his friend, the actor Cary Grant; the notorious London playgirl, Miss Christine Keeler, whose affairs had helped bring down a government; Lady Anne Harley, the grand old dowager who, when she wasn't resting at her Bermuda estate, was pretty much a permanent resident at the Savoy.

Jack Cogan, the handsome thirty-three-year-old recently

appointed to head his father's newspaper empire, was accompanied by his wife, Tiffany, the popular talk show host he had married at the same time as he acquired control of his father's empire. Already his ruthless, take-no-prisoners reputation had earned him the nick name, Jackal.

Also present was the Lloyds banker, Nick Quinn, short and rotund, with his equally short and rotund wife, Katherine; the American novelist Norman Mailer, who had appeared to be already a sheet or two to the wind by the time he arrived. Mailer had written an American bestseller, but he was more famous—or infamous—for having stabbed his wife using a penknife. His wife refused to press charges.

Unshaven, his greying hair a mass of unruly curls, his shirt untucked, Mailer walked into the Pinafore Room and stared in bleary disbelief at the nautical décor lifted directly from Gilbert and Sullivan's fourth operetta. "What the hell is this?" he demanded of no one in particular.

"Good taste, Savoy style, old boy," said Welles, shaking Mailer's hand. "In case you missed the production of *HMS Pinafore*, here before you is the set reproduced—with a nice view of the Thames added."

"Jesus," breathed Mailer. "What am I doing here?"

"What are any of us doing here?" echoed Jack Cogan.

"Unless I miss my guess, I'm here because Mr. Welles is looking for money," said the banker Quinn.

"About the only reason we are anywhere," put in Katherine Quinn.

"My husband tells me you tried to kill your wife," Tiffany Cogan said to an attentive Mailer, obviously drawn to her long blond hair and short dress.

"I didn't try to kill her, I simply stabbed her," he replied mildly.

"Do you write about war?" Tiffany asked.

"How did you know?" Mailer looked impressed.

"That's all men write about," Tiffany sniffed.

"War and sex, baby," Mailer said. "After that, what is there?"

"Wives with knife wounds," observed Tiffany.

"A good meal," added the renowned British playwright and wit, Noël Coward, who was accompanied by his friend, Priscilla Tempest, reinstated recently as head of the Savoy's press office. Tonight, Priscilla dazzled in a chestnut-brown velvet party dress with matching tights that showed off the long legs that tended to drive men crazy—or so she was told. By men, naturally. The problem with that, Priscilla mused, was that her legs routinely set off the wrong crazy men. They would never notice the silver Mary Jane pumps she had recently purchased. However, they did notice—usually after the legs—her pale, pixyish features currently framed by her short russet-blond hair restyled that afternoon in anticipation of the dinner.

A slim woman with auburn hair entered. "My goodness," whispered Noël to Priscilla. "It's Christine Keeler."

"I should know more about her," Priscilla said. "But I was back in Canada at the time, and I only vaguely heard about what I vaguely remember was a scandal."

"A scandal that shook the foundations of this country," said Noël in soto voce. "A few years ago, Miss Keeler was the world's most notorious woman."

"It's a description, alas, with which I am all too familiar," said Priscilla. "Although I wouldn't claim world status—yet."

"Christine was discovered carrying on affairs simultaneously with the cabinet minister John Profumo and a Soviet naval officer attached to the Russian Embassy who was thought to be a spy," Noël continued. "The resulting scandal ruined Profumo's career and brought down the ruling Conservatives. Yet here she is tonight, slipping into the room all but unnoticed."

"But you have noticed, Noël," said Priscilla.

"Of course, my dear," Noël said with a sly smile. "I notice most things and remember all things."

This evening Christine was in a sleeveless red sheath tailored to flatter her figure. A diamante choker around her neck completed the chic ensemble. She frowned as soon as she spotted Jack Cogan with his wife and Mailer. "What's he doing here?" she asked with a jerk of her head in the newspaper mogul's direction as Welles greeted her.

"Ensuring good press while I'm in London," Welles said.

"I wouldn't count on it," Christine said. "Not if the way his father's papers have treated me these past few years is any indication. The Jackal runs things now yet they still go after me."

"Serves you right for toppling a government," Welles said.

"Don't underestimate yourself, Orson," Christine said with a catty smile. "If I can do it, you can too."

Alfred Hitchcock waddled in with Cary Grant, who looked every inch…Cary Grant, an impressed Priscilla quickly decided. Cary took immediate interest. "Are you an actress?" he inquired after introducing himself.

"Hardly," said Priscilla. "I work at the Savoy."

"Not changing the bedsheets, surely," said Cary.

"Not for now," Priscilla agreed. "I'm actually in charge of the press office."

"Good, please do your very best to keep the press away from me."

"Usually, it's the other way around," Priscilla said. "The people I deal with crave attention."

"Not me. I'm far too old for craving."

"Cary Grant can never be too old." Did Priscilla sound breathless when she said this?

"Ah, but you see, I'm not Cary Grant."

"You're not?"

"I'm actually Archie Leach. People keep telling me I'm this strange character named Cary Grant. But I don't believe them."

They were interrupted by Hitchcock, his round porridge face set in an expression of impatience. "There you are Hitch," Cary said, turning to the director. "I want you to meet my new friend, Priscilla. She works in the press office here at the Savoy."

"Enchanted," Hitchcock said in a disinterested voice.

"Hitch loves publicity—and blondes, although not necessarily in that order."

"Cary, I am most displeased with you," Hitchcock said in the slow measured Essex drone that was his trademark.

"Oh? Why is that, Hitch?"

"Spending time with this young woman when you should be listening to me as I convince you to star in *Topaz*, my next film."

"You see, Priscilla, no matter how hard I try, they simply won't let me retire."

"Why should you retire?" Priscilla asked.

"Because I'm far too old to be kissing young women like yourself on a big movie screen."

But what about off the big screen? Priscilla thought before she could stop herself.

"What do you think?" Cary asked Priscilla. "Should I do Hitch's movie?"

Priscilla was momentarily speechless, not sure what to say. Here was one of the most famous stars in the world, even though he had not made a movie in several years, still remarkably handsome, and he was asking her if he should make a movie with Alfred Hitchcock. She was about blurt out, "Of course you should," when Cary cut in.

"There you go," he said with a decisive nod at Hitchcock.

"My new friend Priscilla doesn't want me to do it."

He squeezed Priscilla's arm gently and gave her a wink that weakened her around the knees. Cary was distracted by the entrance of a tall, imposing man with a shock of white hair. "My goodness, it's Louis Mountbatten," Cary said enthusiastically. "Haven't seen him for years."

He made a beeline for Mountbatten. Noël leaned over to speak into Priscilla's ear. "My goodness, this is a crowd. Now we have the former Viceroy of India, the fellow, depending on your point of view, who either brought about the country's independence or sold the British Empire down the Ganges River."

Close by, Cary shook Mountbatten's hand. "Well, this is a pleasant surprise," Mountbatten said. "I didn't know you were even in town."

"A short visit," replied Cary. "How are you, Louis?"

"Oh, you know, soldiering on, I suppose," Mountbatten answered somewhat morosely. "Putting out various fires along the way. What about you, still making those films are you?'

"I keep telling everyone I'm retired. No one seems to believe me—except perhaps for my new friend, Priscilla." He guided Mountbatten over to Priscilla. "Have the two of you met?"

Mountbatten gave Priscilla a speculative look. "I don't believe we have." He took Priscilla's hand. It was a clammy hand, she thought fleetingly.

"A pleasure to meet you, Lord Mountbatten." Was it? Gazing into Mountbatten's cold, expressionless eyes, Priscilla couldn't resist an involuntary shudder. What was that all about? she wondered.

"Miss Tempest is at the Savoy's press office," Cary explained. "She's sworn to protect me from the press."

"I wish someone could protect me from the damned press," Mountbatten said solemnly.

Orson came over. "Louis," he boomed, "delighted you made it. I was beginning to wonder."

"I'd love to tell you the affairs of state delayed me, Orson. But it was the bloody traffic."

"You've arrived just in time," Orson said. "We're about to get started."

"Ah, Noël there you are," Mountbatten said, as Noël joined them. "I religiously scan the Queen's lists in search of your name and your ascension to a knighthood."

"A fruitless search thus far, I fear," replied Noël.

"Not long now, old boy, not long now."

"Have you met my friend, Priscilla?" Noël asked, the excuse to change the subject.

Mountbatten trained those cold eyes on her. "Yes, everyone seems to want me to meet Miss Tempest. Why do you suppose that is Miss Tempest?"

"I imagine it's part of my job, Lord Mountbatten. Meeting everyone, ensuring they are comfortable here at the Savoy."

"Hmmm," was all Mountbatten said before he turned abruptly away.

"I don't think Lord Mountbatten likes me," Priscilla whispered to Noël as guests found their places, indicated by elegant little name cards positioned near the Henning Seidelin cutlery, crafted especially for the Savoy.

"I don't believe Lord Mountbatten likes anyone these days," Noël opined. "The world has passed him by and he doesn't like it one bit. Also, if what I'm hearing is true, Louis is doing a lot of bed hopping and that's potentially getting him into trouble."

"What does his wife think of his bed hopping as you call it?"

"She's doing a fair amount of hopping herself."

"That's a good deal of hopping."

"It's love among the upper classes," stated Noël. "If you're not sleeping with someone you shouldn't, you're not in fashion."

Noël was glancing around as he spoke.

"Is something wrong?" Priscilla asked.

"No, no, it's fine, a silly little thing really," he said, fidgeting with his ever-present cigarette holder.

"Noël!" boomed Orson Welles, from his position at the head of the table. He waved the cigar in his hand around to indicate Priscilla. "You have failed to introduce me to the lovely creature you are with."

"May I present Miss Priscilla Tempest," stated Noël with a wicked smile. "Miss Tempest keeps the champagne flowing in the Savoy's press office."

"It seems you make still more friends, Miss Tempest," Mountbatten observed from across the table.

"I hope I may add you to my list, Lord Mountbatten," Priscilla said.

A thin, unconvincing smile was Mountbatten's only response.

Orson rose to his feet, a majestic figure in a white dinner jacket, a great bearded whale, Priscilla thought, the twenty-five-year-old genius who had made *Citizen Kane*, now grown old and gone grandly fat.

"I would now welcome you all to the Pinafore Room and express my delight that you are here—especially you, Louis. An honour."

"A pleasure, Orson," Mountbatten said. "Even if you are looking for money."

"Mr. Quinn, I don't want you getting the wrong idea," Orson called to the banker at the far end of the table.

"I understand, Mr. Welles," Quinn retorted cheerfully. "I'm always a very popular fellow at these affairs."

"Until he says no," added his wife.

Amidst a rumble of laughter, Orson said, "No money talk tonight, though. Alas, we are missing the man in charge of finances, my producer, Harry Alan Towers, who had to cancel at the last minute."

"Excuse me, Orson," interrupted Noël, a note of concern in his voice, "but am I then to assume that there will be only thirteen guests for dinner tonight?"

"That is correct," Welles said, slightly perplexed at having surrendered to Noël his audience's undivided attention.

"There is the matter of the curse," said Noël. Priscilla shot him a quick look.

"Curse? What Curse?" Welles's porcine face had settled into a frown.

"The curse of the Savoy, old chap," explained Noël calmly, as if a curse at the Savoy was a well-known fact.

Welles arranged a look of amusement "Do explain to us what the devil you are talking about."

Priscilla hoped Noël would back away at this point but she failed to take into account his overweening ego—or perhaps it was the gravity of his subject that made him feel it was necessary to provide an explanation.

"In 1898—" Noël began.

"The year you checked into the Savoy," put in Hitchcock.

"I arrived a year or two later," Noël allowed. "But in that year, a South African millionaire named Woolf Joel hosted a dinner party in this very room. Two of Joel's guests cancelled at the last minute and thus there were thirteen for dinner. As the evening wore on, the conversation turned to various superstitions, including the unlucky number thirteen."

"A rather harmless superstition," suggested Lady Anne Harley, in her plummy rasp of a voice, finally making her presence known. Her late husband was Lord Desmond Harley. The Harleys traced their roots back to Sir Grenville Harley who made his fortune in the slave trade.

"Not entirely true," Noël demurred. "The origin of the ill luck surrounding the number thirteen has been around forever. It is Judas, the thirteenth guest, who arrives at the last supper and betrays Jesus."

"But what has that to do with the Savoy?" asked Mountbatten.

"The reverse of the last supper actually," Noël went on. "It is not the guest who arrives, but the one who leaves. That guest, the curse goes, will meet a terrible fate."

"That's so silly," scoffed Lady Anne. "Whoever heard of such a thing?"

Hitchcock appeared uncustomarily animated as he spoke up: "There is Norse lore that says the evil and chaos of the world was first introduced by the terrible god Loki when he attended another dinner party, this one in Valhalla. Loki happened to be the thirteenth guest."

"At the time, Mr. Joel, the South African host, dismissed any notion of a curse," Noël went on with his typical equanimity. "He proceeded to demonstrate its fallacy by leaving the dinner first—claimed he had to board a cruise ship and return to Johannesburg. However, soon after arriving home, Woolf Joel was shot dead."

The guests were silent. Welles puffed on his cigar. Across the table, Cary Grant cast a doubtful glance at Alfred Hitchcock, sitting like a pale Buddha.

Noël waved around his ivory cigarette holder, as though revving up to continue. "It might have ended there, but it didn't. Within the year four other guests at that dinner, two from here in London, one from Istanbul, and another from Lisbon, all ended up dead under mysterious circumstances. The news of a possible curse made the papers. The Savoy management at the time was understandably concerned that the superstition might actually be real. Or at least of concern for guests. Thus, for years afterwards, if thirteen guests were present in this room for a meal, a fourteenth person was added, often one of the waiters."

"Terribly awkward," observed a scornful Lady Anne. "Introducing a complete stranger into an intimate dinner—and a *waiter*. Goodness gracious."

"Precisely," Noël said. "Thus, the management devised a rather unique solution."

"And what solution was that?" asked Orson Welles, arranging to sound bored by Noël's hijacking of his dinner.

"A cat," Noël said with satisfaction.

"That's a good deal of hopping."

"It's love among the upper classes," stated Noël. "If you're not sleeping with someone you shouldn't, you're not in fashion."

Noël was glancing around as he spoke.

"Is something wrong?" Priscilla asked.

"No, no, it's fine, a silly little thing really," he said, fidgeting with his ever-present cigarette holder.

"Noël!" boomed Orson Welles, from his position at the head of the table. He waved the cigar in his hand around to indicate Priscilla. "You have failed to introduce me to the lovely creature you are with."

"May I present Miss Priscilla Tempest," stated Noël with a wicked smile. "Miss Tempest keeps the champagne flowing in the Savoy's press office."

"It seems you make still more friends, Miss Tempest," Mountbatten observed from across the table.

"I hope I may add you to my list, Lord Mountbatten," Priscilla said.

A thin, unconvincing smile was Mountbatten's only response.

Orson rose to his feet, a majestic figure in a white dinner jacket, a great bearded whale, Priscilla thought, the twenty-five-year-old genius who had made *Citizen Kane*, now grown old and gone grandly fat.

"I would now welcome you all to the Pinafore Room and express my delight that you are here—especially you, Louis. An honour."

"A pleasure, Orson," Mountbatten said. "Even if you are looking for money."

"Mr. Quinn, I don't want you getting the wrong idea," Orson called to the banker at the far end of the table.

"I understand, Mr. Welles," Quinn retorted cheerfully. "I'm always a very popular fellow at these affairs."

"Until he says no," added his wife.

Amidst a rumble of laughter, Orson said, "No money talk tonight, though. Alas, we are missing the man in charge of finances, my producer, Harry Alan Towers, who had to cancel at the last minute."

"Excuse me, Orson," interrupted Noël, a note of concern in his voice, "but am I then to assume that there will be only thirteen guests for dinner tonight?"

"That is correct," Welles said, slightly perplexed at having surrendered to Noël his audience's undivided attention.

"There is the matter of the curse," said Noël. Priscilla shot him a quick look.

"Curse? What Curse?" Welles's porcine face had settled into a frown.

"The curse of the Savoy, old chap," explained Noël calmly, as if a curse at the Savoy was a well-known fact.

Welles arranged a look of amusement "Do explain to us what the devil you are talking about."

Priscilla hoped Noël would back away at this point but she failed to take into account his overweening ego—or perhaps it was the gravity of his subject that made him feel it was necessary to provide an explanation.

"In 1898—" Noël began.

"The year you checked into the Savoy," put in Hitchcock.

"I arrived a year or two later," Noël allowed. "But in that year, a South African millionaire named Woolf Joel hosted a dinner party in this very room. Two of Joel's guests cancelled at the last minute and thus there were thirteen for dinner. As the evening wore on, the conversation turned to various superstitions, including the unlucky number thirteen."

"A rather harmless superstition," suggested Lady Anne Harley, in her plummy rasp of a voice, finally making her presence known. Her late husband was Lord Desmond Harley. The Harleys traced their roots back to Sir Grenville Harley who made his fortune in the slave trade.

"Not entirely true," Noël demurred. "The origin of the ill luck surrounding the number thirteen has been around forever. It is Judas, the thirteenth guest, who arrives at the last supper and betrays Jesus."

"But what has that to do with the Savoy?" asked Mountbatten.

"The reverse of the last supper actually," Noël went on. "It is not the guest who arrives, but the one who leaves. That guest, the curse goes, will meet a terrible fate."

"That's so silly," scoffed Lady Anne. "Whoever heard of such a thing?"

Hitchcock appeared uncustomarily animated as he spoke up: "There is Norse lore that says the evil and chaos of the world was first introduced by the terrible god Loki when he attended another dinner party, this one in Valhalla. Loki happened to be the thirteenth guest."

"At the time, Mr. Joel, the South African host, dismissed any notion of a curse," Noël went on with his typical equanimity. "He proceeded to demonstrate its fallacy by leaving the dinner first—claimed he had to board a cruise ship and return to Johannesburg. However, soon after arriving home, Woolf Joel was shot dead."

The guests were silent. Welles puffed on his cigar. Across the table, Cary Grant cast a doubtful glance at Alfred Hitchcock, sitting like a pale Buddha.

Noël waved around his ivory cigarette holder, as though revving up to continue. "It might have ended there, but it didn't. Within the year four other guests at that dinner, two from here in London, one from Istanbul, and another from Lisbon, all ended up dead under mysterious circumstances. The news of a possible curse made the papers. The Savoy management at the time was understandably concerned that the superstition might actually be real. Or at least of concern for guests. Thus, for years afterwards, if thirteen guests were present in this room for a meal, a fourteenth person was added, often one of the waiters."

"Terribly awkward," observed a scornful Lady Anne. "Introducing a complete stranger into an intimate dinner—and a *waiter*. Goodness gracious."

"Precisely," Noël said. "Thus, the management devised a rather unique solution."

"And what solution was that?" asked Orson Welles.

www.ingramcontent.com/pod-product-compliance
Lightning Source LLC
Chambersburg PA
CBHW031228260626
47169CB00007B/2203